The Dan Trilogy
Book 2

The West,s Awake

James Kilcullen

James Kilcullen

The West's Awake

First edition: March 2018

©Editorial Calíope
©The Dan Trilogy
©The West´s Awake
©James Kilcullen

ISBN: 978-84-17233-42-6
ISBN Digital: 978-84-17233-43-3

Editorial Calíope
Grupo editorial Max Estrella
Calle Fernández de la Hoz 76
28003 Madrid

editorial@editorialcaliope.com
www.editorialcaliope.com

Blessed are the arrogant for they shall become ever more arrogant.
Cursed are the humble for humility is highly overrated.

The tourists came in their thousands; they all wanted to see Rath Pallas; left alone, they would have trampled all over its majestic grassy crown. Ulick and Paulo thought long and hard about it: they wanted the tourists, but not at the expense of disturbing the Little People and destroying the Rath. So, they set up an exhibition hall - and café - in Conna, and lined its walls with hundreds of photos of the airport that was, with a special video section that included coverage of the aborted take-offs, and the magnificent fireworks display.

Then, they engaged Ned McCann - a one- time council employee, not that anyone ever caught him working - to paint a white line across the road one mile from the Rath. Now, whatever happened - only Ned knows the true story - if he does - the straight white line turned out to be a crooked green and yellow line - wavy best describes it - all of one yard wide? Ulick and Paulo viewed this work of art with a mixture of disbelief and horror - as Paulo described it "You could get sea sick just looking at it" but they weren't going to pay him to do it again.

So, they erected the following sign at the side of the road:

To pass this crocked line, if thou not a local be,will earn seven long years of bad luck, for thee.

Visitors were warned "Whatever you do, don't cross Ned's line" and regaled with dire tales about the few that had ventured. Ned could be found in any one of the town's three pubs: telling awe struck tourists how the king of Rath Pallas, himself, no less, appeared that fateful day, drew the line with chalk and instructed him to use green and yellow paint. The more porter they plied him with the more wondrous the tale became.

Ulick built a fine bungalow out the Maam Cross road. On long summer evenings he loved to sit on the high ground above the river; listening to the gurgling, musical sounds of the rapids; the evening breeze rustling in the tall trees; while the noisy crows settled down for the night. He lived there with Nodie in, what he thought, was perfect harmony; their sex life was great but she didn't want to get married.

9

He hoped that, in time, she would change her mind, but he wasn't reading the signs.

Nodie, much as she loved Ulick, felt she had to prove herself: she had lived in his shadow for too long. Perhaps, it would have been different if they had children. Invited to become Circuit Court judge for the south east region, she decided to accept. She knew Ulick would never leave his beloved Connemara: she also knew this would be the end of a very happy relationship. She found it very painful; maybe, after some time apart they could be together again. But life is not like that.

Ulick was surprised and deeply hurt; he knew she had been somewhat moody for some time and put it down to those strange things, known as hormones that women suffer from: men too! He felt he could have persuaded her to stay but it wouldn't be the same. It was over; he accepted it gracefully. When the time came, he offered to drive her to Wexford, where she had bought an apartment. She declined, but agreed to let him drive her to the station in Galway. There, they parted tearfully.

Ulick devoted his time to his constituency work. He took on Marty Walsh, a newly qualified solicitor from Roundstone to help him run his growing legal practice.

Nan, that shrewd little woman, Paulo's partner, decided he needed a house keeper, and kindly agreed to select someone suitable for him. She did; her own niece; a young widow from Carna with no attachments. Ella Rowan was a very attractive brunette with deep brown eyes and a refreshing sense of humour. When she was sixteen, her mother persuaded her to marry John Rowan, a much older man who had a good farm of land overlooking the bay. According to local gossip in Carna, he wasn't up to the job. He died suddenly ten years later leaving her the farm, which she sold and gave most of the proceeds to her widowed mother.

Nan's approach came at the right time; Ella wanted to leave Carna; her big ambition was to become a master chef; the move to Conna suited her; she immediately enrolled in the cookery class at the local technical school. When qualified, she planned to open her own restaurant and bakery in Conna or Galway. In the meantime, looking after Ulick, who spent four days a week in Dublin when the Dail was sitting, was a very agreeable task.

Ulick became very fond of his cheerful, surprisingly frank companion. There was talk, of course; there's always talk in Conna. Emma went about her cookery classes and took no interest in local chit chat. The fact that she dressed so tastefully was duly noted. It was also noted that Emma didn't go to confessions in Conna; she wasn't the only one.

Ulick found himself looking forward to coming home to Ella. She presented him with tasty meals, and the house was always perfect. On winter evenings, when she wasn't at class, they would sit by the fire and chat. He could feel the sexual tension between them but was certain she didn't share it; after all, he was ten years older than her.

Ella admired Ulick long before she came to work for him. He was well known throughout the west as a man of integrity and honour, without any airs or graces; a plain man, modest about his many achievements. She fell for him on day one but, while he was relaxed and friendly, he didn't appear to be interested. Maybe he still loved Nodie: Nan thought that was long over. Ella read up on political matters, and often surprised him with her knowledge of the events of the day. But, still, he made no move.

Desperate, she consulted Nan who counselled her.

'You will just have to take matters into your own hands, my girl.'

***

Great events in history usually have humble beginnings. Ulick attended the Dail regularly; a member of the government party - the FF - said to be the party of honest rogues or cute hoors - depending on who you were talking to - very often, by some of their own supporters. As a back bencher he carried no weight in the party; in truth, he had no interest in party politics; he just wanted the west to get its fair share of the action. That wasn't happening.

The oil refineries in Aran and Achill were processing millions of barrels of crude while he and his colleagues along the western seaboard were fobbed off with empty promises. He thought seriously of resigning, and getting out of politics altogether; that would have pleased the well dressed, arrogant ministers swanking around the country with their Mercs and perks while the civil servants made the decisions and did all the work.

He had secured a promise from Minister Jack Carey; the new fish processing factory would go to Westport where it would provide two hundred badly needed jobs. However, as time passed and nothing happened, a rumour circulated around Leinster House to the effect that the new factory was going to Cross Haven in Cork. He sought a meeting with the minister; ten days later the minister condescended to see him.

He was shown into the palatial ministerial office in Kildare Street, where Minister Carey was seated behind a large mahogany desk, with his civil servant sitting beside him. Young, brash with clear cut features the minister waited impatiently while he demanded to know what was happening. It was clear the minister regarded back benchers as an undesirable - if necessary - form of low life.

When Ulick finished his remarks, the minister deferred to his civil servant; an elderly bored looking man called Mick O'Mahony who kept looking at his watch.

'Deputy Joyc,' the civil servant opened his file. 'We've had to re-evaluate this contract. The Cork location is more suitable because it's nearer to continental markets.'

'Bullshit.' Ulick replied looking straight at the minister whose expression suggested he wished he were elsewhere.

O'Mahony persisted. 'I assure you, deputy that our experts have studied this matter in great detail.'

'Bollocks.' Ulick replied angrily. 'Do you see any wisps of straw sticking out my ears? Where better to site this factory than in the minister's constituency, with a bye election in the offing?'

The minister was clearly horrified by the usage of such language.

'Deputy Joyc,' he tried to sound patient, 'this was a cabinet decision. As you well know our majority in the house is seriously under threat.'

Ulick got up. 'It'll be under more than threat by the time I'm finished.'

He stalked out of the room and headed for the Dail bar where he ordered a pint of Guinness. Frank Carney, the TD for Mayo - a member of the FG opposition party - the party that occupied the high moral ground (so they said) - was there before him. They had worked together to get the factory for Westport. Ulick's angry expression told him all he needed to know. There were few deputies in the bar at this hour. He ordered a pint for Frank; they sat down together in a quiet corner.

Frankie Carney and Ulick were old friends, and met regularly in Paulo's pub in Conna for a few pints.   A young looking sixty Fank was a stocky, strongly built, follicily challenged - as they say these days - farmer with broad features and steel grey eyes. A widower, he lived in Louisburg with his young blonde partner, Lisa; his two sons had emigrated to Australia after they qualified as doctors at Galway University.

Quick witted, a rarity for a politician - a TD for thirty years - his sarcastic tongue was like the crack of a whip. An old friend of Ulick's father, John Joyc, a leading TD for Galway, he served in the Dublin Parliament with John until his untimely death.

They sipped their pints in silence for a while.

'What can we do?' Frank asked eventually.

'The choice now is: walk away or do something really radical.'

'What have you got in mind?'

'How do the rest of the western TD's feel about being totally ignored when it comes to getting our share of the action?'

'They're fed up, coming up here, week after week, to be herded like sheep through the voting lobby.'

Ulick paused for a minute.

'Would they be prepared to form a separate region within the USE?'

'I'm sure they would jump at the idea; but could we do it?'

'We qualify on economic grounds. I believe Brussels would approve it.'

'Are you sure?'

'I talked with Alf O'Reilly who is a senior executive in Brussels; he doesn't think there would be a problem provided a majority of our people vote for it. Alf is from Castlebar.'

'Do we qualify on population numbers?'

'We do if we take Donegal, the five counties of Connaught, Clare, Limerick, Tipperary and Kerry.'

Frank did a few figures in his head.

'That gives us sixty four TDs. How would we go about it?'

'I think we should call a meeting of the sixty four and seek their support.'

'Wouldn't Taoiseach Matt Cotter get to hear about it?'

'I'm sure he would.' He paused. 'The important question is: will the people of the west back it?'

'They'll jump at it.'

'Right. Will you talk to your colleagues; I'll talk to mine and the independents. We'll call a secret meeting for three weeks time in Galway.'

'It won't be secret for long.

***

Momentous events were taking place in the enlarged United States of Europe, or USE, as it was now called. It had expanded too rapidly, bringing in countries totally unprepared to make, even the minimum contribution required. Too many demands on the common purse, added to the usual fraud and corruption, led to a disastrous fall in the value of the Euro. The USE was threatened with financial collapse which would have led to its disintegration.

At an emergency meeting of the heads of State, it became clear that only one man could save the situation, Count Otto Von Vernher, the German Premier. But, as in all things in life there was a price to pay. To provide the necessary funds and assurances to save the USE, he insisted that he be appointed President with dictatorial powers. They had no option but to agree: it was that or nothing. Afterwards, it was incorrectly said that the Count helped bring about the crisis to achieve his own ends; he merely took advantage of it.

Count Otto, as he was known, was a big man in every respect, with a great big head, ruddy features and a large bald dome. Although nearly fifty, he exercised every day in his specially built gymnasium at the Von Vernher Castle in Friedrich's Haven overlooking Lake Constance. A marksman, skilled swordsman and horseman, he hunted regularly and prided himself on his prowess and physical fitness. He inherited the magnificent old castle from his late father, together with the largest privately owned business Empire in Germany. His passion being politics and power, he appointed a board of Trustees to manage the family trust. Particularly proud of his ancestry, he could trace his lineage back to an illustrious Prussian Chancellor (so he said) in the nineteenth century.

The immediate effect of the Count's appointment was staggering; he was thought to be a pragmatic politician although little known outside Germany. Now, he became an absolute dictator, circulating all kinds of directives without consultation. The Premiers of the member states couldn't believe the change: their views were simply swept aside; he refused to take their phone calls. Absolute and immediate compliance was demanded. The various offices of the USE were left in place to carry out his instructions. Most of the senior executives were replaced with his own appointees; their only required qualifications being absolute obedience to him.

Von Vernher Castle became the official Head quarters of the USE. He rarely visited any of the Commissions; the Parliament was suspended for the duration. Those close to him suffered his sudden mood swings, and ill tempered rages, with well tried patience. He dismissed his attractive wife Honoria and daughter Eva; they went to live in her father's mansion near Hamburg. For the past two years, they had not even been invited to Von Vernher Castle for official functions.

Count Otto's father, Hugo had a distinguished military and business career. His wife died after fifteen years of marriage leaving him with identical twin sons - Otto and Gunter. They were brought up by a very severe governess; competed fiercely with each other in sports and outdoor activities, often coming to blows. Their father, in failing health, employed two tutors to educate them. Otto was more academically minded and quickly developed an interest in Politics. Joining the Democratic Party, he eventually became Prime Minister, before the crisis in the USE, which led to his present exalted position.

Gunter was a wild and unpredictable young man and, as time passed, it became obvious he was mentally unstable. He loved beautiful women, fast cars, champagne and brandy and even learned to fly a Cessna plane. He was always in trouble, whether it was crashing cars or the Cessna, which he crashed once - or brawling. A Von Vernher, he believed he could do as he pleased. Fortunately, he didn't marry. It became very embarrassing for his father who wanted to believe he was just sowing his wild oats.

However, something had to be done, when he set fire to a local inn that refused to serve him. Everything was covered up quietly; he was kept under guard at the family's estate on the island of Mainau. Well treated, and kept in relative comfort, he was quietly airbrushed out of the family history. But he was very cunning and managed to escape twice. Otto used to visit him regularly but his last visit was so stormy that he was advised to stay away.

***

The meeting took place in the banqueting hall of the old Railway Hotel overlooking Eyre Square in Galway. As convenors, Ulick and Frank sat at the top table; all sixty four deputies attended. Ulick could see that most of them appeared to be a bit apprehensive.

When they quieted down, he addressed them.

'Thank you all for coming here tonight. We may be from different parties, but we all have one thing in common: the determination to look after the people of the west. As things stand, thanks to the Dublin bureaucracy, we're unable to do that. Briefly, what Frank Carney and I are proposing is quite simple: that we, as public representatives for the ten counties, recommend to our electors that we break with the Dublin Government and set up a separate state within the USE. It's in the best interests of our people; it's financially viable; we qualify under USE rules: all we require is the approval of our electors by way of referendum, and the agreement of the Dublin Government. This meeting is now open to you.'

Nora O'Donnell - Donegal - rose. 'How do we know the people of the west will support this idea?'

Ulick smiled - good question. 'Nora, we have carried out a survey: 90% of the people are with us.'

Ned Harte - Leitrim - rose. 'Wouldn't this be a massive task; setting up a new state from scratch? I cannot see how it would work.'

Ulick smiled - Ned was a well known cynic.

'We thought that earlier: then we discovered we already have an almost complete infra structure in place. We have our county councils to deal with local matters; our courts; our police, even a small army detachment, not that we'll need one.'

Mary Higgins - Clare - rose. 'What about our social services, Ulick, pensions, social welfare, unemployment?'

'They're already dealt with from Sligo for the entire country. We can re-programme the computers to cater for our state only and let Dublin make their own arrangements.'

Moxy O'Shea - Kerry -rose. 'Dublin will never agree.'

Frank replied to him. 'They will if we go about it the right way.'

'But we would have to have a capital, a parliament, a government, civil service, a flag and a national anthem,' Moxy responded.

Ulick smiled. 'Let's take one step at a time: we know the people approve. I'm now asking you to approve by way of a show of hands.'

He watched while the hands went up - slowly at first - showing all in favor.

'Good. Now, we can get down to details. Before we leave here tonight, I suggest that we elect a provisional Government.'

Frank raised his hand.

'I would like to propose that Ulick Joyc be our first Taoiseach.'

The crowd roared their approval. Before anyone could second the motion, Ulick rose.

'Thank you for your support but I'm not a candidate for any position in government.'

They gasped in surprise; Frank's face registered his disappointment, although Moxy O'Shea looked quite pleased.

Ulick continued.

'As soon as we achieve our objective, I want to take life a bit more leisurely. Before we elect a provisional Government, I'd like to make a few remarks: I believe we need fewer ministers than Dublin; each appointee should be approved by a majority of the members; I believe we should serve our electors - not a party system.'

He was interrupted by John Marren - Sligo. 'I'm disappointed, Ulick, that you won't accept the position of Taoiseach. Will you, at least, remain as our leader until we break with Dublin?'

'I'll do that. Now, before I ask for nominations, we need to decide on the number of ministries we require.'

***

Two nights later, Ulick and Frank met for a few pints in Paulo's pub in Conna. The press had picked up the story and the gang of "sixty four" - as they were now known - was in receipt of dire threats from the main party leaders. They sipped their pints quietly for a while. Paulo, as usual, was busily polishing glasses trying to contain his curiosity. Ulick looked quite pleased; Frank didn't.

'The bastards got a full report of our meeting; we've all got our marching orders.'

Ulick smiled. 'That's exactly what I wanted: they've fallen into my trap; expelled the lot of us, except the independents, of course.'

Frank shook his head in disbelief. 'It was you tipped off the press?'

'Of course. By taking such drastic action they probably thought they could frighten us into subjection; in fact, they've united us as never before.'

Paulo put up two more pints. 'Those are on the house, lads: those fellows in Dublin don't know what they're up against.'

'They'll know come Tuesday,' Frank promised.

***

In preparation for the showdown with the Dublin Government, the provisional Government worked through the weekend on outstanding matters. Frank wasn't impressed when Moxy O'Shea was elected Taoiseach but agreed not to oppose him provided Galway would be the Capital. The new state would be named "Hibernia." The number of ministries was set at seven; each minister would be entitled to a maximum of ten civil servants. Frank was elected Minister for Industry, Tourism and Land.

They agreed to adopt the Republic of Ireland constitution, suitably amended. Moxy would lead the delegation to Brussels. This would be a rare experiment in informality. There would be no political parties; no Mercs; few Perks; no Senate; no Presidency; no spin Doctors. Ministers would have to compose their own speeches. Frank remarked. "We'll have very short speeches from now on."

The owners of the hotel agreed to lease it to the new government, and convert the banqueting room to an assembly hall. This would be known as "Teac Galway" and the deputies would now be called "TGs" - Teacta Gaillim. To emphasise the spirit of democracy the chamber would be set out in a large circle with seats upholstered in green, the speaker's chair in red.

***

Ulick arrived home unexpectedly early one afternoon - Ella knew he was coming - to find her sitting in an armchair in the living room, with book in hand, wearing a loose pink negligee over satin lingerie, her shapely legs in full view. She jumped up pulling her negligee around her. He couldn't take his eyes off her as he moved closer.

'Sorry, Ulick, I wasn't expecting you so early.'

'Ella, you're so lovely.'

She stood a little closer, with her head slightly tilted and looked up at him with that vulnerable expression in her big brown eyes that no man can resist.

'What are you going to do about it, Ulick?'

He took her in his arms.

***

Provisional Taoiseach, Moxy O'Shea, a solicitor by profession was an artful, consummate politician. He could talk all day without saying anything; he didn't have to look into his heart to know the people wanted the soft options. When asked a really unwelcome question, he would smile broadly, and say "Now, I'm glad you asked me that" and proceed to answer a totally different question.

A pleasant looking, little man in his forties, with twinkling blue eyes and florid features, he made a point of dressing well, but modestly. The people liked that. To his enemies, he was a conniving, calculating, crafty son of a sheep farmer from Sneem in Kerry. That didn't bother him.

He was married to Joan, they had three grown up daughters, and lived in a fine bungalow overlooking the bay. A pillar of society, he escorted his wife to Mass every Sunday morning and, on occasion, even did some of the readings. Known to take an occasional pint, he was the essence of a genuinely committed servant of the people: but some of his constituents knew otherwise; not that any of them would dream of giving scandal about one of their own.

He had made it to the top and he intended to stay there. Under USE conformity rules, he knew that only the title Premier would be accepted; he had no problem with that. But he had concerns about two members of the Teac; Ulick Joyc and Frank Carney. Carney could have been Premier if he so wished. A blunt, sometimes abrasive, culchie (a thick to those who don't know the Gaelic) he was not to be underestimated. Joyc was a man who didn't want power for himself; such men are dangerous - they tend to have principles, and principles have no place in politics. Moxy's agile brain was already working on a plan to sideline Joyc.

He smiled to himself; his colleagues were very surprised he accepted, after a show of great reluctance, Galway as the Capital of the new state. He agreed with some of his disgruntled constituents - Killarney was the obvious choice - but, as he explained to them, he couldn't deliver everything. After all, didn't Kerry have the honour of having the first Taoiseach of the new state?

No, Galway was much more suitable for him. He would have to overnight there and was already looking to buy a nice new apartment out in Moycullen overlooking Lough Corrib. When in situ, he would bring his secretary cum mistress - the beautiful, young brunette, Helen Moore - down from Dublin and install her in his new pad.

***

On Tuesday morning, amidst a blaze of publicity, Ulick drove to Dublin accompanied by Frank. The Taoiseach, in a televised address, made it quite clear that there was no way Dublin would ever agree to release its west of Ireland territory to a bunch of country yobs who didn't know their asses from their elbows. He put it more politely than that, but everyone knew what he meant.

The gang of sixty four assembled in the Shelbourne Hotel. Ulick was pleased to see they were all there: local support on the ground was so favourable to the idea of a new state that it would have taken a very courageous deputy to change her mind. Together, they walked down Kildare Street to the Dail where a large, curious crowd greeted them affably. Clearly, they thought it was a great joke. Approached by media people they agreed to pose for a group photo but Ulick refused to be interviewed.

He led his troops through the front doors of Leinster House, up the wide blue carpeted stairway to the chamber. The other one hundred odd deputies were there before them; some darting very hostile glances in their direction. The ushers looked very confused; they didn't know where to seat them. Ulick led his deputies down on to the floor of the House where he spoke to the head usher.

'Don't worry about seating; we'll stand here.'

He looked around; the visitors' galleries were full to capacity.

The Taoiseach tried to ignore their presence.

He rose. 'Madam Speaker, as agreed with the party whips, we'll take the vote on the Budget now.'

Ulick raised his voice. 'Ceann Comairle, please suspend the rules of this house so that I may propose a very important motion.'

The Taoiseach rose. 'Madam Speaker, we have no notice of any such motion.'

Ulick replied calmly.

'Madam Speaker, this is a unique occasion; I must respectively insist that we be recognised by the House, seeing it is now governed by a minority government.'

The Speaker, an elderly lady looked distinctly uncomfortable.

She addressed Ulick.

'Deputy, I realize that the rules of this house do not cater for this type of eventuality. I will, therefore allow you to make a statement to the house but I will not permit a debate at such short notice.'

Ulick smiled.

'Thank you, Madam Speaker. I don't need to dwell on the official statement that has already been submitted to the Taoiseach setting out our entitlement - more importantly, the entitlement of our constituents - to a separate state. It is our earnest wish that we leave this assembly, for which we have the highest regard with your blessing and good wishes. There will be many situations in the future when co-operation on both sides will be essential. And you will all be very welcome when you visit our state on holidays.'

His followers applauded.

The leader of the opposition, John Reilly, from Cavan, rose; he stood to gain from the departure of so many government deputies.

'Madam Speaker, I would suggest to the Taoiseach that this house adjourn until 2.30 this afternoon to allow time for private discussions between the Taoiseach, Deputy Joyce and myself.'

The Taoiseach looked uncertain for a moment, then realized he had little choice.

He rose. 'Madam Speaker, I accept the deputy's suggestion. We will now adjourn until 2.30 this afternoon.'

The Speaker looked relieved. 'The house will now adjourn until two-thirty this afternoon.'

***

They sat down together in the Taoiseach's office. Coffee was served and they were left alone. The Taoiseach was visibly angry.

'This is a bluff, Joyc; what do you want? A ministry?'

Ulick smiled. 'What we want Taoiseach is the blessing of Dail Eireann.'

John Reilly had to be seen to support the status quo.

'Ulick, you haven't got the infra structure to set up a separate state.'

Ulick took two typed pages from his inside pocket and handed them one each.

'I think you'll find we've done our homework.'

They perused the list for a few moments.

The Taoiseach put it down.

'Where are you going to get a High Court, a Supreme Court, or a police commissioner?'

Ulick smiled. 'We're going to take them from you. Ten of the High Court and Supreme Court judges are from the west and the Assistant Garda Commissioner is from Tipperary.'

'They won't leave their present positions.' The Taoiseach blustered.

'Have you asked them? We have.'

John Reilly sat back.

'It seems to me, Ulick, that your ideas are not as half baked as we thought.'

The Taoiseach thumped the desk.

'You will never get the consent of Dail Eireann.'

Ulick looked at the leader of the opposition.

'What do you think?'

John Reilly had only been leader of his party for less than a year and had little to show for it; the vultures were already starting to circle. He could see a whole range of possibilities here provided he retained Ulick's support.

'Are you sure, Ulick, that the people of the west will support you?'

'Yes, we wouldn't proceed without that assurance; we'll be holding a referendum in ten days time.'

Satisfied he had Reilly's support, Ulick pressed on.

'Taoiseach, we would really like to leave Dail Eireann on amicable terms; I believe the country would want that.'

The Taoiseach had no difficulty doing the figures: if FG voted with Joyc - he knew he couldn't trust Reilly - his government would be voted down. It would lead to an immediate and very divisive general election: something to be avoided at all costs.

'Well, gentlemen.' He paused. 'It looks as though the people of the west have made up their minds to leave Dail Eireann.' He paused again. 'Subject to that being established by way of referendum, I will agree to the setting up of the new state.'

Ulick rose and shook hands with both of them.

'History will be made in Dail Eireann today: thank you both.'

***

The setting up of the state of Hibernia was approved by 96% of the people of western Ireland; followed, two days later, by the formal authorisation from Brussels. Amidst great celebrations and excitement throughout the west the new government met in Galway to prepare for the opening of Teac Galway.

***

Ulick was having a few pints with Ozzy when they were joined by Frank who had just come from a cabinet meeting in Galway. Frank had met Ozzy on a few occasions, but didn't know him very well and wondered why this oddly dressed, somewhat simple Connemara man, was so highly regarded by Ulick. Pints pulled and paid for, Frank sat with them.

'Ulick, we need to talk.'

He smiled. 'Frank you may talk freely in front of Ozzy.'

'Very well.' But he didn't like it.

'Under our Constitution we have to have a President.'

'I thought we left that out.'

'So did I, but it's still there; maybe it has something to do with these new USE conformity laws. Anyway, the cabinet wants you to be our first President.'

He sipped his pint. 'What does the President do?'

'Fuck all except sign bills into law. In the event of a national emergency the President becomes all powerful.'

'That doesn't sound too serious; would I still be a member of the Teac?'

'No. We'd have to have a bye election to fill your seat.'

'Is this Moxy's way of getting rid of me?'

'I believe so but I think you should take it.'

'Why?'

'You would also be chairman of the Council of State: a very powerful position where you could ride herd on the wily Moxy. He's already started talking about getting a fleet of Mercedes, for official business, of course. I'll take care of that one.'

Ulick looked closely at him. 'You could have been Taoiseach: why didn't you take it?'

He nodded to Paulo.

'I'm getting on a bit in years. I prefer to let the younger members to the work.'

Ulick turned to Ozzy, who stayed silent during this exchange.

'What do you think? Should I become President?'

'I think so.'

'You could be my aide-de-camp.'

24

'What's that?'

Ulick smiled. 'You would have to accompany me on state occasions.'

'Would I have to wear a uniform?'

'No, you'll do fine as you are: this is a slightly democratic state.'

Frank didn't know where to look.

***

The great day dawned at last: when the new state of Hibernia came into being and the members of Teac Galway would meet, in formal session, to commence work on behalf of the people. Eyre Square was decorated with multi coloured bunting; thousands of happy, cheering, singing people - young and old - packed into the square and adjoining streets. Ten bands, wearing their county colours, marched down Bohermore playing "Galway Bay" "The Rose of Tralee" "Moonlight in Mayo" "The hills of Donegal" and "The West's Awake." They were followed by the TGs, led by Ulick and Moxy; members of all county and borough councils; a large force of Gardai; representatives from the universities, secondary and national schools; members of all denominations of local clergy; a large contingent of doctors and nurses; an army detachment; representatives from Industry, Farming, Fishing and Business; followed by ambulances, fire brigades, civil defence; a large number of performers in colourful costumes; and then the people - in their thousands.

The entire event was broadcast live on HB TV. The TGs lined up for photos outside the Railway hotel. Then, when the bands stopped playing, a mike was handed to Ulick; a great roar went up; this was the man they all wanted to hear.

He smiled. 'Welcome my friends, proud citizens of the new state of Hibernia.' He had to stop when a great and prolonged roar erupted from that massive crowd. He continued. 'Relax; I'm not going to make a speech today. You are all very welcome here, on this, the inauguration day of your new state. Your TGs will now formally commence work on your behalf. I wish them well.' He paused for a moment. 'Let us show the world we can make a success of running our own affairs.'

The people cheered; the bands played; it was still going on when the TGs entered the Teac thirty minutes later.

***

The main business that first day was to approve the Constitution; it was expected to go through on the nod and then be put to the people. Moxy, delighted that Ulick wasn't a member of the Teac, was a bit wary of Frank Carney. The Teac came to order.

Frank Colgan frowned as he read slowly through the document. Then recognised by the Chair he rose.

'Comairle.' He always used the Gaelic version. 'I see here that the ownership and control of our most valuable assets, namely the Aran and Achill oil and gas fields will pass to the USE if this Constitution is approved. I can't support any such Constitution, and recommend that it be rejected by the Teac.'

The other TGs rushed to examine the wording. Disappointed, Moxy rose. His theory of keeping mine enemy close wasn't working.

'Madam Speaker, we're still negotiating with the USE on a number of matters and, at the very least, expect to receive all oil revenues. In the meantime, the Count insists that we approve this Constitution.'

Frank rose again. 'Comairle, I can't go along with this. I am resigning as Minister, and will continue to totally oppose this Constitution in its present form.'

A number of his colleagues cheered and four more of the new Ministers resigned.

Moxy rose. 'As your elected Taoiseach, I propose that the Teac approve the draft Constitution. If you reject it, I will have no option but to resign as Taoiseach.'

He knew he was taking a big gamble, but few would want to be seen to be forcing a General Election at this early stage.

Frank called for a vote. The motion was carried by 32 votes to 31.

So, in the finest Irish tradition, they now had the "Split" and, despite all the good intentions, the evil of party politics hadn't gone away. The circle was broken.

Frank rose. 'When this Constitution goes to the people there will be a different result.'

Moxy breathed a sigh of relief. He had survived and could put off that evil day for quite some time. But an ever greater problem had appeared on his horizon: one that could blow him and his supporters out of the water.

***

There was always mystery and intrigue about Turla Lodge, or Turla Lodge Hotel and Abbey, as it was now called and much depended on which version you believed, if any. Some said it was built by a Spanish nobleman in the nineteenth century; apparently, he needed to get lost. He landed in Galway with a trunk full of gold, selected the magnificent site in Maam Valley and built his fine cut stone castle there. Others believed it was an English patriot turned pirate (or pirate turned patriot) who disappeared conveniently from Liverpool shortly after a large quantity of gold went walk about. Whoever it was they picked a beautiful site with Lough Turla in the foreground and the wooded mountains of Maam rising steeply behind the sprawling castle. It was said there were underground escape tunnels and a disused silver mine under the mountains. The forecourt, now a large car park, was decorated with a number of marble, nude Greek beauties. The building itself was mostly three storied with ten acres of walled gardens at the rear; in the centre a tall square turret dominated.

Whatever its history, the last owner left during the Great War and never returned. It lay derelict for more than ten years before it was purchased by an order of monks called the Fathers of the Brothers. Fifty monks, mostly Spanish and Italian, moved in, tried to upgrade the interior and started growing fruit and vegetables in the gardens. The locals relaxed when it became obvious the newcomers were not intent on converting the good people of Connemara. So, they treated them with due respect and left them alone. As the years passed, the older monks went with them and were replaced, mostly, by locals. They became part of the background of Connemara.

Then, early in the twenty first century a new Abbot, Brother Meskedra arrived to take charge. A fine, handsome, dark haired man with brown eyes, he sported a well trimmed beard. Soft, manicured hands indicated a career that did not include manual labour. He said he came from the Father house but no one could recall having ever heard from the Father house. He provided a detailed account but became a bit vague when asked where it was.

Now Lurglurg, the fifty three year old current Abbot, was so happy to be relieved of his responsibilities he wept with joy. No longer would he have to worry about where the next meal was coming from.

A big boned, bald man with large square features, his expression was somewhat mournful, and he spoke usually in direst tones.

Born and reared on a small holding on the Aran Island of Inish Mor, he worked on the building sites in London for a number of years. When his mother died suddenly, he came home and stayed to help out his father. Being an only child he expected to inherit the farm. When his father married again, he left and worked for a year with the Turf Board in Connemara.

Here he came in contact with the brothers in the Abbey and joined two years later. He loved the land and would have happily spent the rest of his days showing his fellow brothers how to produce the finest fruit and vegetables; but they had different ideas and elected him Abbot. It was a job he didn't want, but couldn't very well refuse. He now looked forward to spending more time in the gardens.

Abbot Meskedra surveyed the castle and surrounds before calling a meeting of the brothers. They sat down together around the big, old, wooden table in what they called the refectory.

'Brothers, what is the purpose of our order?'

Old brother Ned, crippled with rheumatism, spoke up.

'To help the poor, Abbot.'

Lurglurg added in a mournful voice.

'We are the poor.'

The new Abbot smiled. 'Exactly, so therefore, we have, first of all, to look after ourselves.'

'How can we do that?' Brother Ned inquired.

'Brothers, I'm going to turn this mausoleum into a luxury hotel.'

He waited for comment. Lurglurg, in calmer moments, wondered how the new Abbot could know so much about him and many of the brothers before he arrived. He had no complaints. Mysteries were not for him. Eventually he spoke up.

'Abbot,' he asked respectfully, 'Where are you going to get the money?'

'I'll get a loan from the bank.'

Lurglurg tried to hide his dismay. He couldn't even get an interview with the Bank Manager.

'You're the Boss, Abbot.'

From there on, he was known to the brothers as the "Boss" a title that amused him.

He borrowed millions and entirely refurbished the castle; added a leisure centre, skilfully concealed at the rear; employed extra staff, and advertised extensively in the American market. The turret was fitted out as a luxury apartment for his own use. He had 150 rooms for letting. Soon the tourists began to arrive in large numbers.

They were astonished to find so many beautiful, young female staff, adorned rather than dressed, in very fetching white and red uniforms. When one American lady questioned the suitability of such attractive ladies in an abbey, the boss smiled and retorted. 'The good Lord never said there was anything wrong with temptation: wasn't he tempted himself?'

She persisted. 'But when do the brothers get time to say their prayers?'

'Madam,' he smiled politely, 'Work is prayer, and I can assure you our brothers work all hours.'

All of the brothers were provided with new uniforms more in keeping with their revised work schedule. They looked very smart in their blue shirts with brown trousers, and sandals to give some slight recognition to their vow of poverty. Some of the older brothers who worked downstairs, or in the gardens, objected. Being a liberal Boss he allowed them to continue as before. In order, as he said himself, to give good example he always wore a fine brown woollen habit tied around his waist with a white cord. Tempted, as he was, he didn't add the traditional long black beads.

***

The original owner obtained a Charter from the British Crown permitting him to distil Poitin, a local brew that could easily be mistaken for paint stripper. However, there was attached a condition that prevented him selling the brew, although he could make as much as he liked. This Charter still attached to the current owners; the Boss examined its possibilities. He inspected the large old, worn out distilling plant in the basement, used only to make sufficient Poitin for the brothers.

Lurglurg was astonished when a Dublin firm arrived one day with a modern distilling plant, and installed it in the basement, taking away the old one. Meskedra examined the distilling formula and decided they would have two brands for the future. One would be PPS or Pure Pot Still, and the other would be PD or Pure Dynamite.

Now, Lurglurg was so baffled by all this, to the point that he had the audacity, as he saw it, to question the Boss.

'Lurglurg,' he smiled, 'under no circumstances are we going to sell Poitin. We're going to install a box in Reception with the word "Offerings" on it. If anyone would like some Poitin; they should put an offering in the box; enter the amount of the offering in the book provided; the size of the offering will dictate the quantity of Spirits they may expect.'

He shook his head in admiration.

'Pure genius, Boss.'

'Pure spirits, Lurglurg.'

'How are we going to have two different brands, Boss?'

'Did I say two different brands? Oh, yes. What I mean is, we'll have two different labels, and the PD brand will require a more substantial offering.' He paused and grinned. 'This will be our little secret; the brothers will receive only the best brand.'

'But won't people notice there's no difference between the brands?'

'If they do, you merely point out that it takes a connoisseur to appreciate the difference.'

That was good enough for Lurglurg, although he didn't know what a connoisseur was.

'It was God himself sent you, Boss.'

He smiled. He liked Lurglurg; he could work with him and, if he had queries about the new Abbot, he kept them to himself.

'We should inform our suppliers of our willingness to regard their purchases as offerings: that would enable us to reward them with some of our finest brand.'

'Can we provide Poitin to our in-house guests?'

'Of course, it's free of charge. You can include a suitable offering in the room rate.'

'What about yourself, Boss?'

'I'm strictly a Brandy and Cigar man.'

'I've instructed one of the waitresses to look after your needs.'

'That was very kind of you, Lurglurg. Are the brothers happy with the changes?'

'Oh, yes, Boss, especially the introduction of variable vows.'

'We are a somewhat Christian order.'

The good people of Connemara watched the extraordinary changes that Meskedra brought about. Some approved, some were outraged, but all were fascinated with the activities of a Christian order that did not appear to be in communion with Rome, or anywhere else for that matter. As time progressed he added coach tours - including a special trip once a week to view Ned's line - boating and fishing on the lake, with an occasional pilgrimage to Knock thrown in, to satisfy the truly devout.

Now six years later, with the setting up of the new state, Meskedra looked forward to even greater numbers of American tourists. He would be disappointed.

***

Standing, looking out of his office window at the lively activity in Eyre Square below, the Taoiseach, Moxy O'Shea, was worried; and not without good reason. He fought many battles in the past but this problem just wouldn't go away and, if he got it wrong, he and his party would be swept out of office. He looked at his watch. Senor Maldini, the Italian Commissioner for Conformity in the USE, would be calling on him shortly.

There was a polite knock on his door; his secretary, Helen Moore - now ensconced in his new apartment in Moycullen - showed in Enrico Maldini, an immaculately dressed, rotund, swarthy Italian, with big brown eyes, who smiled while they shook hands.

'You are very welcome to Hibernia, Enrico.'

'Thank you, Premier.' He would have preferred to be somewhere else in view of the message he had come to deliver.

Refreshments were served and they were left alone.

Moxy took up where he finished off at their last unsuccessful meeting.

'Enrico, I would be committing political suicide if I even tried to put this Directive into force.'

He smiled patiently. 'None of the other member states had any difficulty. Why should it be different here in Galway?'

'We're a new state with old traditions; a very independent minded people who don't take kindly to dictation.'

He tried persuasion. 'People have such short memories. Thank goodness.' He waved his hands. 'A little furore; in a short time it's all forgotten. Life moves on.'

'Enrico, I know what the people will swallow.'

He persisted. There were days when he didn't like his job.

'Senor Moxy, like we say in Italia, create a diversion or pass the poisoned chalice.'

'I've already thought of that.'

He shrugged. 'You know the Count, he insists on conformity in all things.'

'Is he god?'

He nodded sadly. 'So far as we're concerned: he is. You can do it. Pick a time when the people are preoccupied with other things.'

'That would be difficult with the community paying our farmers to sit around scratching their arses, not that I object to that.'

He rose to leave. 'Senor Moxy, please try before the end of July. I don't want to be the one who has to report failure to the Count.'

They shook hands. 'I'll see what I can do.'

***

Ulick and Ozzy were having a quiet pint (a modest name for a pint of Guinness with a white frothy head, specially pulled by Paulo and consumed with immense pleasure, in convivial company) when they were joined by Frank Carney.

'Good evening, Mr President, greetings Ozzy and Paulo.'

Ulick grunted, although he was smiling. 'No titles allowed here, Frank. Do you want me to dismiss you from the Teac?' He turned to

Paulo. 'Will you give the leader of the National Party a pint? He looks as though he needs it.'

Paulo pulled three pints.

Frank became serious. 'I don't like the way things are going in the Middle East. The new man in Turkey plans to restore the old Ottoman Empire, and he can do it too. He controls the water supply.'

Ulick agreed. 'It could be his revenge for being refused entry to the USE. It looks like a Federation of Arab states with Israel out on a limb; puts America in a tight corner.'

'That's how I see it. Oil prices are going through the roof. We've got plenty of oil, but according to the big Count it isn't ours.'

Ulick put down his glass. 'It's our oil Frank and the sooner we make that clear to Count Otto the better. When is the Teac adjourning for the summer recess?'

'Next Friday, just before the start of Race Week.' He paused. 'Moxy is keeping very quiet. I wonder what he is up to now.'

***

It was end of term day. The TGs were looking forward to a break. The atmosphere in the house was relaxed and friendly; it was expected outstanding matters would be passed without division. One final Bill was circulated when the Teac came to order. Moxy was all smiles to everyone, but inwardly, holding his breath. Senor Maldini was quite specific when he telephoned early that morning; the Directive must be enforced; the Count would not countenance any disobedience from any member state. Frank Carney looked quite calm, but would he stay that way when the new Bill was introduced by Minister Manny Higgins?

The Speaker addressed them. 'The Teac will come to order.'

Frank rose immediately. 'Comairle, will the Taoiseach tell us why this Bill wasn't circulated yesterday in the usual way?'

'Deputy Carney, kindly address the chair in accordance with the new conformity Directives.'

'Yes, Comairle, now will the Taoiseach answer the question?'

The Speaker gave up. Moxy rose.

'The deputy will realise it's a busy time of year.'

''Tis for hoors, hawkers and knackers.'

The Speaker continued. 'Minister Higgins.'

Frank put on his glasses, and proceeded to examine the Bill; Manny Higgins rose.

'Mr Speaker, in view of the day that's in it, I will come directly to the First Schedule.' He paused and looked around him.

'Be it enacted by Teac Galway that the Weights and Measures Act of 1927, enacted by Dail Eireann be repealed and, from a date to be set by the Minister, all Imperial weights and measures be abolished and replaced by Grams and Litres.'

He didn't get any further; Frank jumped up.

'Comairle, am I hearing right? Is he proposing to abolish the Pint of Guinness?'

'Deputy Carney, please address the Speaker properly.'

'Certainly, Comairle, did I hear correctly?'

'You will have ample opportunity to question the Minister when the full Bill is put before the Teac.'

Moxy's bulk seemed to shrink in his seat, as he realised his worst fears.

Members on both sides of the Teac were sitting up and taking notice.

'Comairle, I'm asking the Minister a simple question that calls for a simple yes or no.'

The Minister tried to kick for touch.

'Deputy Carney, I'm not abolishing the pint; I'm merely replacing it with half a litre.'

Frank waved the offending Bill. 'If you're not abolishing it, why replace it?'

'The deputy will know we have to put through this enactment to comply with the requirements of Directive 43865 of the USE. We have no choice in the matter.'

'Comairle, I call on the Minister to withdraw this rubbish.'

Moxy rose, very reluctantly. 'Mr Speaker, great as my respect is for the Leader of the Opposition he knows as well as I do that we are obliged to fulfil the terms of the Treaty of Paris.'

Frank looked directly at him. 'So, you propose to proceed with this rubbish?'

'Yes, deputy.'

Frank held the floor.

'Comairle, our forefathers endured hardship; oppression; execution; deportation; degradation; deprivation and famine to achieve our freedom from the world's most powerful empire of the day. And what did we do with it? We delivered ourselves, bound and gagged to the big Count who will decide what we'll eat and drink and when we'll eat and drink. It's time to call a halt, here and now: Captain Boycott only took our land.'

Moxy rose again. The die was cast now. He couldn't withdraw.

'Mr Speaker, as loyal members of the USE we have to obey the rules like every other mation. The Minister will continue to read the Bill.'

Frank was incensed. 'Comairle, the first duty of the members of this Teac is to the people who elected us. The Taoiseach may have enough boots on his side of the Teac to force this rubbish through; the people have boots too, and when the time comes they will know how to use them. I am now leaving this Teac.'

He rose and was followed by many of the deputies to the steps outside where he held an impromptu press conference in which he roundly condemned this despicable bill. Then, he rang Ulick.

Moxy now had another worry. Would the remaining deputies support the measure? There was widespread dissatisfaction among the deputies. He sat there for another hour until the rest of the Bill was put before them. Then, to his great relief the Bill was passed by 32 votes to 31. But he was wise enough to know it wasn't all over yet. He personally rang the President to ask him to come to the Teac to sign the Bill into Law.

***

By the time Ulick arrived a hostile crowd had gathered in Eyre Square. He went to his official office, where Moxy explained the position and sat quietly while he read the Provisions of the Bill. He looked disgruntled. Moxy was already thinking ahead: once the President signed the Bill into Law it would become his responsibility. Ulick finished reading.

'Mr President, you could refer it to the Supreme Court.'

'I suppose I could.'

'Their decision wouldn't greatly affect either of us.'

'You've got it all worked out.'

Moxy smiled. ''Tis hard to serve two masters.'

Ulick looked at his watch.

'Can you arrange a TV appearance for the six o'clock news?'

'Of course, I'll have the cameras come here immediately.' He paused. 'Would you like me to appear with you?'

'No.'

At one minute past six, by which time HBTV had alerted the entire country to the day's events, Ulick faced the cameras.

'My friends, I have been asked to sign into Law the new Weights and Measures Bill - abolishing the Pint of Guinness - or refer it to the Supreme Court. I have decided to do neither. I am referring the Bill to you to decide by way of Referendum. Your decision will bind the Teac. I know it's not usual for the President to make a recommendation but this matter is so crucial that I'm recommending rejection.'

***

Commissioner Enrico Maldini was perspiring freely when he was shown into the Count's gymnasium, where the great man was removing his safety gloves, having completed his daily fencing exercise. His exhausted opponent bowed and departed hurriedly; doubtless relieved he wasn't run through by the angry Count, who now turned his attention to the quivering Maldini.

'This fellow, what's his name, actually refuses to obey my directives?'

'Joyc, sir, yes, sir.'

'Dismiss him immediately, he should be horse whipped. I'll send someone to take charge of this place. What's it called?'

'Hibernia, sir.' He paused and cleared his throat apologetically. 'We can't do that, sir.'

'Why not? I can do whatever I like.'

He swished his rapier before the red faced commissioner's nose.

'It would look bad, sir. I mean, wouldn't it be better to summon him before the Council of Ministers and make a public exhibition of him?'

'Oh, all right then. Order him to appear before us in Paris. Use the Luxembourg Palace. I can't be preoccupied with tin pot dictators with war about to break out in the Middle East.'

'What if he refuses to come to Paris, sir?'

'Refuses, refuses, no one dares refuse me.' He roared. 'I'll send the army to arrest him. You make sure you tell him that. Now get out.'

The quivering, perspiring, commissioner withdrew. It was unnerving dealing with god.

***

After a long and difficult meeting of the Teac, Ulick and Frank met in Paulo's. Ozzy was sitting there sipping his pint, talking to Nan, Paulo's partner. That was necessary because her exact status was a well kept secret, and in Conna, you don't ask questions unless you already know the answer. And if you know the answer, why ask the question?

Nan turned to Ulick. 'How is Ella?'

He knew that she knew about his love affair with Ella; he also knew Nan and Ella were very discreet not that discretion ever bothered him.

He smiled. 'She's fine, Nan. I hear you're both going to the fashion show in Galway tonight.'

'We are that; Ella has a good eye for style,' she paused and smiled mysteriously.

'As you well know.'

He grinned nodding.

'I see you're in the news again; that big Count needs to learn some manners.'

Frank agreed. 'How right you are, Nan and Ulick is the man to do it now that a state of Emergency has been declared and he's in charge.'

Ulick grunted. 'This is not something I ever wanted but we have to fight for our rights.' He turned to Ozzy who was listening quietly.

'I have been summoned to Paris. Will you come with me?'

Frank looked surprised but said nothing.

Ozzy grinned. 'Would that be an order, President?'

'Yes, Ozzy.'

Frank added. 'I'm going too.'

Ulick shook his head. 'No, I want you to keep an eye on things here. It's me the Big Count wants and it's me he shall have.'

Ulick could see that Ozzy's presence puzzled Frank. He took him aside when they were alone and explained his friendship, in confidence, with the little man from the Rath.

***

Meskedra sat in his usual armchair inside the front window in Reception, and watched another group of Americans check out early. It was his custom to sit here for two hours every afternoon. A glum looking Lurglurg saw them off and then joined him.

'More departures?'

Lurglurg nodded. 'Threats of war in the Middle East and we're the first victims.'

A very pretty, young waitress approached carrying a tray, and offered a large brandy and cigar to Meskedra.

'Thank you, my child,' he smiled while Lurglurg lit a match and helped incinerate the cigar.

Knowing the Boss's liberal philosophy he was surprised that none of the young beauties was ever invited to his luxury apartment in the tower. It was an unkind thought on his part; and he knew it; he should be surprised, to be surprised at anything the Boss did or didn't do.

Meskedra sipped his brandy. 'The Bank Manager won't like this.'

'Do we owe much?'

'I borrowed several millions to convert this old castle into a hotel.'

'What's to become of us, Boss?'

He smiled reassuringly. 'Don't worry, I'll think of something.'

'Our variable vow of poverty might have to become permanent.'

He paused. 'Brother Sean is behaving as if our variable vow of chastity is meant to be a permanent vow of fornication.'

Meskedra watched an official looking gentleman enter reception and approach the desk.

'I hope not, but to be a true Christian is to be a great sinner. Would it help if we reduced his Poitin ration?'

'We'll have to reduce something.'

The official looking man - with a document in his hand - left the desk and stood before the boss.

'Abbot Meskedra?'

He nodded silently.

The man pressed the document into his reluctant hands. 'I serve on you a summons to appear at the Galway Circuit Court where his Lordship Bishop Brennan will seek an order for the possession of this property and estate. Do you understand?'

The Boss pulled a crumpled card from an inside pocket and showed it to the man. It read "At this time, I am bound by my variable vow of silence and may not offend by having intercourse with anyone."

The stranger grunted and left. Lurglurg became very worried.

'Can he do this, Boss?'

'He can try. It seems the first abbot may have been conned into signing a document to that effect. I believe the order paid for this estate with its own funds.'

Lurglurg departed to check the Poitin offerings. The Boss never ceased to amaze him; he consumed only one brandy in reception; he rarely drank in his apartment; and, starting at seven every morning, he worked out for an hour in the gym. If he prayed at all - not a matter of any concern to the brothers - he did so in the privacy of his apartment. All very confusing to a simple soul like Lurglurg who believed that Viagra was a waterfall.

***

Ulick and Ozzy took the scheduled Air Hibernia flight to Paris, despite Frank's efforts to persuade him take one of the airlines executive jets. Moxy saw them off at the airport; quite pleased that he was no longer in the line of fire. As soon as the big Count sorted out Ulick, he would resume his role as Taoiseach and all would be well with the world again.

***

At Charles De Gaulle airport, they walked, unnoticed, past a large number of media people who were expecting an impressive delegation. They were approached by a foppish, long haired, artistic looking youngish Frenchman.

'Welcome to Paris, Mr President. I'm Sam Maguire, my mother came from Clifden. I serve the best Guinness in France.'

Ulick smiled as they shook hands; this fellow would cause some excitement out Clifden way.

'Where is your pub, Sam?'

'Just around the corner from the Elysee Palace. Any taxi will take you there.'

'We'll visit you later. First the Luxembourg Palace. Have you any idea where it is?'

'I'll drive you there myself, sir.'

***

Ulick's visit to Paris was front page news. The Count's spin doctors let it be known that the meeting would be shown live on USETV: it would be no contest - Joyc would comply or be dismissed on the spot. A large crowd gathered to watch the line of Mercedes cars draw up outside the palace, and deposit the various USE country leaders and Commissioners.

Then, a black Mercedes, in the middle of an armed convoy, drew up and heavily armed guards took up positions around the entrance. The big Count alighted, was surrounded by his guards - ignored the crowd - and walked briskly into the Palace. Finally, Sam Maguire, driving his old yellow Volkswagen, dropped Ulick; he walked slowly towards the entrance where he was met by a friendly young secretary.

'President Joyc?'

'That's me.'

'Kindly follow me, sir.'

He looked around in awe at the beautiful Gothic architecture of this old palace; led down a long corridor, lined with world famous paintings, he stopped outside the hall of Justice. Opening the door the secretary stood aside.

Ulick entered the great hall and looked around him. There was a long mahogany table - a long way away - with the big Count sitting in the middle on one side, flanked by about fifty sombre looking heads of states and Commissioners: dressed so formally it appeared they were attending a funeral. On the other side of the table, to which Ulick was led, there was only one lowly chair, so low in fact that had he sat on it his head could barely be seen above the table. He noticed there was a jug of water and glass in front of those sitting on the other side, but none on his side. Clearly, he was to be intimidated. A uniformed lackey politely indicated the chair. The TV cameras zoomed in on the new arrival.

'Thank you, I'll stand,' Ulick glanced at the Count sitting confidently across from him.

He was to be regarded as the prisoner in the dock; in truth, he felt like it too. Those surrounding the big Count stared at him in silence.

Count Otto began. 'I have summoned the President of Hibernia here because he and some of his people do not seem to understand that in these United States of Europe there must be absolute unity of mind, purpose and practice.' He paused. 'I therefore, call on President,' he paused (his secretary whispered something in his ear) 'Joyc, to undertake to comply with all USE Directives.'

There is a murmur of approval from his side. Ulick took the Count's angry stare, but his mouth was dry; he needed a drink.

He addressed them calmly. 'Gentlemen, my people have rejected Directive 43865 by a massive majority. In so far as we are concerned, that is the end of the matter.'

The big Count roared at him. 'You have no choice: sign the Bill - to give effect to our directive - here and now or I'll dismiss your Government and rule by decree.'

Ulick tried to stay calm. 'I haven't come here to hear any threats against my people.'

He looked to his left, and it was immediately clear to those present or watching that he was buoyed up by whatever was happening. Seen only by Ulick, Dan strode briskly towards the table with his hands behind his back, and a very vexed expression on his usually benign countenance. Climbing up on the table, he walked along it staring at the line-up against Ulick.

He then stood between Ulick and the Count and pointed at the stern looking people surrounding the Count.

'They look like rejects from Madame Tussaud's.'

Ulick smiled.

Dan pointed at the lowly chair; to everyone's astonishment it started to grow. When it was higher than the Count's, it stopped. Those present gasped. Ulick smiled and sat down, but he was still very thirsty.

Lifting the Count's water jug and glass, Dan placed them before Ulick who filled the glass and drank most of its contents. There was absolute silence. How did the jug and glass float from one side of the table to the other? Was it an optical illusion? The TV resorted to action replay to show millions of viewers that it actually happened. The big Count just sat there and stared. Dan lifted the jug, walked across the table and holding it high above the Count's head began to tilt it forward slowly.

'No, Dan,' Ulick begged.

Disappointed, he lowered the jug and placed it in the middle of the table. A servant refilled it, and tried to place it before the Count; no matter how hard he tried Dan wouldn't let go. He gave up. The Count stared angrily at the jug. Dan sat beside it with arms folded and legs crossed.

The Count was prompted by his secretary.

'I'm not impressed by your illusions: sign the Bill or I will apply direct rule to your country.'

Dan shook his tiny fist at him.

Ulick was feeling a lot better now. 'Count, it's good of you to acknowledge that it's still our country. My people were long civilised when yours were still running, bare arsed, before the Romans. We've seen off bigger empires than yours. Do not even think to attack us; today, you have seen only a small sample of our powers: we have secret weapons more powerful than anything your scientists have even dreamed of. Do not force us to use our Padmisiles.'

The Count saw red. Rising suddenly, he grabbed the jug and pulled with all his might. Dan held tight, smiling at Ulick. The Count was committed, he wouldn't let go. The tussle was being watched by millions of fascinated viewers. Ulick smiled.

Then, a mischievous look appeared in Dan's eyes.

'Oh, well, if he wants it that badly, let him have it.'

He released his grip suddenly. The jug flew up, its entire contents dashing into the big Count's face.

Dan danced around the top of the table, clapping his hands in delight.

'I knew he would, I knew he would. I haven't seen anyone that angry since Attila the Hun.'

Dan looked at the serious expressions of the Count's colleagues and turned to Ulick.

'I told you: they're dummies.'

The TV people ignored the frantic signals to get off the air. Throwing aside the jug the Count leapt up and roared. 'Arrest that man.'

Dan grinned, as he grabbed Ulick's hand. 'Oh, Oh, time to go.'

Millions of viewers blinked when Ulick disappeared.

A strange look appeared in the Count's eyes; he looked around him warily. Had he seen what he thought he saw? The tiny little voice in the back of his head asked the same question. Could he be going like Gunter? Then his secretary spoke in hushed tones.

'He's just disappeared: that's not possible.'

As guards searched the hall the big Count roared. 'Find him, don't let him escape.'

***

In Paulo's crowded pub in Conna, there was a great cheer.

Paulo smiled happily. 'Dan is on the job. He'll soon sort out that big Count.'

Frank was thinking ahead. 'With a stalemate in the Middle East, and no oil being produced there our oil reserves are becoming more important by the hour.'

Paulo agreed. 'That might explain why the American Ambassador is looking to meet you.'

'The big Count is hell bent on a trade war with the Americans. With control of most of the world's oil supply, he would hold all the aces.'

Paulo protested. 'But it's our oil, Frank.'

'We have to make sure it continues to be our oil. Fill another pint there when you have a minute.'

***

When Ulick eventually arrived at Sam Maguire's pub he received a great reception from cheering customers: they didn't like the big Count either. Ozzy was there to meet him. It has to be said that Ulick wasn't surprised.

Ozzy smiled as he greeted him. 'Mr President, what will it be?'

'We'll have two pints, Sam.'

'Two pints coming up, sir, and two fingers to the big Count. It's been a long time since the people of Paris got such a laugh.'

He raised his voice and mimicked the Count "Arrest that man."

Police sirens sounded nearby; coming closer, getting louder, six cars pulled up outside; and several policemen raced towards the pub. Sam reacted quickly; lifting the trapdoor to the cellar, he yelled.

'Mr President, Ozzy, hide down here, quickly now.'

Taking their pints, they clambered down the steps and found themselves in a large, well stocked, darkened cellar. They could hear the furore above. Ulick and Ozzy became separated in the darkness. The trapdoor was opened and the lights came on; Sam could be heard protesting loudly. Six policemen clambered down the steps, while Ulick backed away towards an old brick wall.

"We ave im," one shouted to someone above.

They lined up to charge Ulick. At that instant, Dan appeared beside him, took his hand and pulled him through the wall into an adjoining cellar. The policemen charged into the wall; falling backwards on top of one another using very undiplomatic language.

'Whew, that was close,' Ulick gasped, 'What do we do now?'

'We go home. Count, bad man.'

Dan took him by the hand, and together they made their way to the street where they walked through a cordon of policemen. They joined a large crowd of tourists heading towards the pleasure boats on the Seine nearby. Ulick sneezed and let go of Dan's hand to get his handkerchief. He was spotted immediately by a policeman who yelled "There he is."

Unseen, hand in hand again, they walked on to the boat and eased their way forward towards the bow. The intrigued tourists were unceremoniously pushed aside when a large number of policemen clambered aboard. Dan took two life belts off their hooks and threw them into the river. They stood back and watched while the Police Chief and two of his assistants leaned over the side trying to figure out if the fugitives were escaping down river. Dan's hands positively itched; he stood behind the three bent over figures. Unable to resist the temptation, he pushed them into the dark brown water below.

He clapped his hands gleefully. 'I knew they would.'

While the unhappy police were being rescued, Ulick and Dan headed towards the rear of the boat with a view to slipping away quietly. The tourists were having a great time with their cameras. When Ulick saw the police officers being hauled aboard in such undignified fashion, he started to laugh and was immediately heard by two officers nearby.

"He's here," one shouted angrily.

Dan grabbed Ulick while ten officers formed a circle around them and, with outstretched arms, began to move in. They slipped quietly between the officers who crashed into one another and collapsed on the deck in a pile of bodies; much to the delight of the watching tourists who were now getting their revenge.

Getting off the boat, they headed towards a police car parked nearby.

'Get in,' Dan ordered.

'You can't drive.'

'Me quick learner.'

To get into the car they had to separate.

'There he is,' a policeman shouted running forward.

Dan fiddled with the controls but nothing happened. To the approaching policemen, it appeared that Ulick was sitting by himself in the passenger seat.

Dan became impatient. 'Horses go.'

The engine kicked into life.

He pointed ahead. 'Go that a way.'

The car leapt forward at speed with tyres screaming while angry policemen raced to their cars. Standing on the seat, Dan was enjoying himself; they raced down the Champs De Elysee against the traffic; oncoming cars, swerving to avoid them, crashed into one another. They charged around the Arc De triumph and headed towards the Plaice De La Concorde. Ulick closed his eyes and would have prayed if he knew how. Parisian pedestrians enjoyed the ridiculous sight of a driverless car leading a cavalcade of police cars. By now, all traffic in the centre of Paris had come to a halt; Dan was really enjoying himself. The chaotic, exciting, chase was going out live on international TV.

Ulick eventually got his mind in gear.

'Can we find the airport?'

Dan was a bit reluctant, seeing he was enjoying himself so much.

'I suppose.'

'I'll look for a sign post.'

Round and round they went until Ulick suddenly spotted a sign post for the airport.

'Turn left,' he shouted.

They were practically on the turn, and doing at least a hundred, but that didn't bother Dan. 'Horses, left now,' he yelled.

The car spun around six times, then charged off to the left while its pursuers braked viciously trying to make the same turn; they couldn't and ended up crashing into one another and a fruit and vegetable stand sending apples and oranges flying in all directions. The TV vans fought their way around the pile of damaged cars and continued the chase. Angry policemen abandoned their wrecks, using very bad language, while another squad bypassed them and powered after the fugitives.

Dan drove down the right side of the motorway, not knowing it was the right side and they were soon clear of the centre.

Traffic on the motorway was alerted. Their progress was now monitored by two helicopters hovering overhead.

***

In the Luxembourg Palace, the big Count and his Commissioners were following events on television. His temper had not improved, despite a quick change of clothes.

'Get him, get him, don't let him escape,' he roared.

***

In Paulo's pub, the craic was mighty.

'Good on you, Dan, show them how it's done,' Frank roared with delight.

Paulo followed. 'Ulick, will you smile, you're on TV.'

One of the crowd. "Oh, shit, look at the roadblock coming up ahead."

***

Ulick saw the roadblock ahead.

'What are we going to do now? We can't get past that.'

Dan grinned. 'We go home.'

He increased speed; Ulick closed his eyes. An entire cavalcade of police cars and TV vans followed them. There was no escape but Dan still increased speed. He could see the armed police ahead, looking anxiously at them. Then, two hundred metres from the roadblock, he yelled. 'Up horses, up horses'; the car rose and sailed over the top of the roadblock hitting the road gently on the other side.

Five minutes later, he pulled up outside Departures. Before Dan could intervene, six policemen pulled Ulick out of the car and escorted him into the Terminal building - handcuffed between two officers. He cantered along behind them to the airport manager's office where the irate manager addressed the officer angrily.

'How dare you close down my airport to capture one man! I have twenty flights on hold out there. Can I open it now?'

The officer was quite excited about his captive. 'Yes, you may open it now. We'll hold this man here until the Chief arrives.'

When the mollified manager departed, the officer positively preened himself as he watched the announcement on TV. Ulick, very unimpressed with the rough treatment he received, smiled when Dan entered the office and pointed his index finger at the group; they froze like a tableau. Ulick liked it.

'Get me out of these yokes, lad.'

Dan clicked his fingers and the handcuffs fell to the ground. Picking them up, he handcuffed them all together.

He then took Ulick by the hand. 'We go home now.'

***

The afternoon flight to Galway was climbing out over the North Sea when the unfortunate officers were found in the manager's office. The big Count was livid.

He roared. 'Put up fighter jets. Turn that plane back to Paris. He's not going to get away that easily.'

Captain Eamon Murphy was unaware that Ulick was on board; like everyone else he thought he was in custody. His first reaction to the order was to obey it. Then, he decided to check his passengers, and he was astonished to find his President sitting quietly with Ozzy.

'Mr President, I've been ordered to return to Paris. What should I do?'

'Ignore it, John. I think we had better join you in the cockpit.'

By the time they got there, Ulick saw two jet fighters, one on either side of them. The First Officer was talking to one of the pilots. He stopped and turned to the Captain.

'Captain, they say their orders are to escort us back to Paris. If we refuse, they've been ordered to shoot us down.'

Captain Murphy was livid.

'Are they serious? We've got three hundred passengers on this plane.'

'They don't like it any more than we do.'

Ozzy started to rub the inside of the hull. Suddenly there was a scream from one of the escorts.

'Jaysus, they've disappeared. What the hell is going on here? I've still got them on Radar.'

Ozzy asked Ulick quietly. 'What Radar?'

'It's like a TV screen. There's a blip for every plane in the sky. That's how they track them.'

Ozzy smiled. The escort screamed again.

'Jaysus, now we've lost them on Radar. Have they crashed? What the hell is going on?'

Ulick spoke very quietly to the First officer. 'Break off radio communication.'

The captain turned to Ulick. 'I'd like to know what's going on too.'

'Some day, I'll tell you.'

At that moment, Paris tower tried to contact them. "Paris tower to HIB 563. We've lost you on Radar. Come in please."

Ulick shook his head. The Captain switched off the radio and turned to Ulick.

'Are your friends at it again?'

Ulick smiled. 'I think so. Please continue your present course to Galway.'

Even as he spoke the fighters left them.

'They'll think we've gone down, Mr President.'

'Let them. That's better than being shot down.'

'I can't just fly blindly into Galway. I'll have to contact the tower for instructions.'

'Of course, but wait until we're in our own airspace.'

***

As flight 563 cruised high above the cliffs of Moher, Captain Murphy contacted Galway tower.

"Flight 563 it's some relief to hear from you. We now have you on Radar. We're calling off the air and sea search. Paris TV has accused the Count of having you shot down. Turn right to runway 23. Wind speed – 7 knots."

'The President would like to talk to Frank Carney. Can you patch us through to him?'

'Will do. Mr Carney and Mr O'Shea arrived here twenty minutes ago.'

Ulick couldn't believe the extraordinary welcome that awaited them when they touched down. An hour earlier it had been announced by HBTV that the President's plane had disappeared off radar. It was believed to have crashed.

When the doors were opened, Ulick was the first to step out to be greeted by a great cheer from the crowds on the viewing balcony.

Frank, Moxy and most members of the Teac were waiting on the tarmac. They were furious at the manner in which their President was treated. Ulick smiled as he walked through that festive crowd to the airport board room, to participate in a hastily arranged emergency meeting of the Teac. Bemused passengers, unaware of the drama en route, were astonished to find so many of their relatives and friends gathered to meet them.

Moxy knew this was a time to go with the flow. When they crammed into the board room, Ulick addressed them.

'My friends, we're not going to waste time on today's events. The question is: do we remain in the USE or do we declare our independence?'

Moxy rose. 'Mr President, let me congratulate you on your magnificent performance and safe return.'

Ulick made light of it.

Moxy continued. 'Before we do anything hasty, I believe we should give the Count the opportunity to accept our position.'

There was a murmur of disapproval.

Frank rose. 'I don't think the big Count is for turning. He broke every law of civilisation today. I propose that we resign from the USE and declare Hibernia a sovereign and independent state.'

Moxy intervened. 'Can we afford to go it alone?'

Ulick intervened. 'Have we physical control of our oil and gas refineries?'

Frank nodded. 'We do.'

'Are you sure?'

'I've already checked. They're Irish and with us to a man. From now on they'll take their orders from our Minister for Energy and no other.'

Ulick looked around the assembly.

'We must be absolutely united in whatever we do now.'

Frank rose. 'My proposal should now be put to the vote.'

Moxy was never backward in coming forward.

'I agree entirely and suggest the motion be carried by acclamation.'

And so it was that the motion to leave the USE was passed: by a unanimous majority.

Ulick rose. 'I believe we should set up a national government and ask the people to approve our decision. Now, who is going to inform the Count?'

Frank was up like a shot. 'I'll be happy to inform the big Count and I'll do it in language that even he will understand.'

***

In the Garda barracks in Conna, Sergeant Jack Mulhall, the rotund, middle aged, mild mannered, local Garda chief, folded his papers and prepared to head over to Paulo's for a pint. With the passing of time his job had become more agreeable; he no longer had to deal with sheep stealers in a land where there were, officially, no sheep. The fact that his old friend, Ulick Joyc, was President didn't add to his responsibilities; Ulick wouldn't hear of any form of personal protection.

***

Ulick and Ozzy were having a quiet pint in Paulo's crowded pub, where they were joined by Frank, now Minister for Foreign Affairs.

'Evening Paulo. Another pint there if you please.'

Paulo smiled. 'Yes, Minister, are you not buying one for the President and Ozzy?'

He grunted agreeably. 'I suppose I'd better, otherwise I might get the sack.'

'Have you seen the headlines in the Dublin papers?' Paulo asked Ulick.

'No, I never read the Dublin papers.'

'They're saying you're running a country from a pub.'

'What if we are? It helps to keep the overheads down.'

He turned to Frank. 'Are the results in yet?'

'Yes, 97% of the people are with us.' He opened his briefcase and extracted a document. 'All I need now is your signature.'

Ulick looked over the document put it on the counter and signed it.

Paulo put three pints before them.

'Paulo,' Frank announced proudly. 'We are now a Sovereign and Independent state.'

'Does the big Count know?'

Ulick looked at the TV in the corner where the news was just starting.

'I think he does.'

The Count's big countenance filled the screen.

"No member state of the USE may resign without my permission and I have not given permission to (he consulted his notes) Hibernia. I now formally order the withdrawal of that resignation." He paused and continued angrily. "It is not acceptable in a peaceful democracy like ours that weapons of mass destruction, including chemical and nuclear warheads be under the control of a lunatic despot." He paused and looked at his notes.

"It has come to my attention that an illegal force has taken over our oil refineries in Aran and Achill. I will give the bandits exactly seven days to hand over all their weapons of mass destruction and restore my refineries. Failure to do so will result in immediate military intervention by the USE armed forces."

His angry countenance disappeared from the screen. The news continued.

"We have not yet received comment from President Joyc. Now the rest of the news."

Paulo looked a bit anxious. 'What are we going to do?'

Ulick was unperturbed. 'Tell him to fuck off.'

***

The Count was having breakfast, as always, by himself in his enormous dining room surrounded by some of Picasso's and Titian's greatest masterpieces. He had watched Ulick's formal announcement - on live TV - of the unilateral declaration of Independence. He almost choked on his toast when Ulick asked all free nations to welcome his country into the great family of nations. If there was anything he couldn't stand, it was defiance. Eyes flashing angrily, he thumped the table noisily.

'Butler, butler, where the hell is the man?'

His young brown and white collie dog got out from under the table and scampered out of the room. An elderly, long suffering servant, entered and stood beside his master.

'You called, sire?'

'Yes, I damn well called. Is everyone deaf around here?'

He replied, with an expression somewhere between boredom, resignation and indifference. 'No, sire.'

'Has the Chief-of-Staff arrived yet?'

'Yes, sire, he's waiting outside.'

'Why wasn't I told? Show him in at once.'

'Yes, sire.' He left as silently as he came.

Dan, who had followed this exchange, was very unimpressed; he wandered around the room and ended up sitting on the other end of the long mahogany table. The butler returned, followed by a tall, handsome looking man in a splendid blue military uniform, with lots of impressive looking medals decorating his chest.

He saluted smartly. 'General Antonio Bendes at your service, Count.'

General Antonio Bendes was the first Commander-in-Chief of the USE Combined Armed Forces; he was responsible for all senior appointments in the Army, Navy and Air force. The armed forces of all member countries were now co-ordinated into cohesive USE defence forces. New officer training colleges were set up in London, Madrid and Milan; Naval command was centred in Cadiz and Athens; the air force and nuclear missile headquarters was located near Munich.

A native of Lisbon, General Bendes had seen action as a fighter pilot in Kosovo where he served with distinction. Noted for his organisational skills, he was given the job of co-ordinating the EU air force and, prior to his present command, served as President of the military college in Milan. He carried out his duties in a very professional manner and impressed on his subordinates the absolute necessity to give their full allegiance to the USE. Very much a hands on commander, he spent much of his time visiting his officers and inspecting the troops.

With an enormous budget allocation at his disposal, he implemented a major purchasing programme replacing obsolete national equipment with the most up to date fighters, bombers, missiles, tanks and battle ships. New aircraft carriers were nearing completion in Glasgow and Hamburg.

Although his official Headquarters were in Paris, the Commander spent most of his time in a small executive unit close to the Count's palace in Friedrick's Haven. At forty six, twice divorced, with two grown daughters, he lived with his partner Helga, a very attractive, blonde airline pilot, twenty years his junior. He played a good round of golf and enjoyed sailing on the lake. Although mild mannered and reflective, he was not to be underestimated, as some of his commanders found out to their cost.

He wasn't invited to sit down.

'General, I want the city of (he looked at his notes) Galway destroyed by rockets.'

'But, sire, we can't very well destroy one of our own cities, especially as the American government has now recognised Hibermia as an independent state.'

'This is no business of the Americans. Galway is of no importance. I'm only interested in the oil fields. Do it.'

'Sire,' he cautioned, 'What about the possibility of retaliation? Should we not, first of all, locate and destroy Joyc's rockets?'

'Rubbish, he's bluffing. There are no rockets. If there were I'd know about them.'

'But in your TV address you said?'

'Never mind what I said in my TV address.'

The general looked distinctly unhappy. 'Sire, the US President says that any attack on Hibernia will be regarded as an attack on the US.'

'The petticoat President hasn't the guts to go to war with me.'

'May I say sire that I think this action would be contra productive.'

The Count roared at him. 'General, you are not paid to think, you are paid to obey. Do it.'

The unhappy C-in-C saluted and withdrew.

Left alone a crafty gleam appeared in the Count's eyes. War with America. That's exactly what I want.

Dan shook his little fist angrily at him. 'You bad man, I fix ya.'

***

C-in-C Bendes was taken by helicopter to the underground silo near Munich, unaware he was accompanied by Dan who was very vexed indeed. Leaving the helicopter, the Commander was escorted to a lift that descended thirty floors to a large open area with line after line of rockets in launch position. Twenty computer operators manned a bank of computers at one end of the area. The Commander talked with an older man, called Kurt, with grey hair and glasses, who seemed to be in charge here.

Dan stood behind the operatives trying to figure out what this strange computer business was all about. It was all double Dutch to him until he put his hand gently on each operative's hand. Then, it was quite simple. Most were tracking satellites; some controlled the launch and guidance of missiles; others operated a system to destroy rogue missiles.

The Commander was talking persuasively to the man in charge who was extremely angry.

'Is he mad?' he demanded.

'Probably, Kurt,' he conceded, 'but we have to carry out his orders.'

'We're not at war. I'm not launching any missiles with nuclear warheads.'

'Well then, use conventional explosives.'

Exasperated, he gave in. 'Oh, all right but you have to instruct me in writing. I'm not taking responsibility for this.'

The Commander handed him a prepared written instruction.

'I hope you've covered your ass.'

He took a small tape recorder from his pocket, and held it up.

'I'm going to sit on this for twenty four hours to give that lunatic time to come to his senses.'

'Do it tonight.'

***

Ulick liked Abbot Meskedra; he had charisma. Here was a man who could make a success of any role in life yet he chose to be a simple man of the cloth; not that there was anything simple about Meskedra. Ulick was convinced he wasn't always a brother, but enquiries about his earlier life were, invariably met with a mysterious smile. He acted for the order when Meskedra raised a large loan from the Lynch

Bank in Galway. He had doubts about Meskedra's ability to persuade the bank to lend him so much money; Meskedra had no such doubts, and surprised everyone by making a great success of the project.

Ulick was friendly with Pat McDermott, the bank manager, and on one occasion chided him gently about his confidence in this extraordinary man of the cloth. Pat smiled enigmatically and remarked "I wish I had more clients like the Abbot." This did little to satisfy Ulick's curiosity about the man that introduced variable vows in Connemara and operated an interesting version of a philanthropic Poitin distillery.

Bishop Barney Brennan, known locally as BBB, was sometimes described as big Barney Brennan although he was a rotund little man in his late forties. Something of a dandy, and a pompous one at that, he cultivated an accent that the natives did not know, dyed his hair black, nourished his sagging features and expected and usually received the homage due to a king. But his deep blue eyes were cold and, despite his repeated exhortations to the faithful to seek the kingdom of Heaven, he had his own two feet firmly planted on this earth.

He didn't show any interest in the Fathers of the Brothers until Meskedra arrived, and transformed the Abbey into a highly successful venture. He then decided the Order came under his control and instructed Meskedra to report to him with an up to date copy of the accounts. He was politely informed that the order held a private Charter from Pope Pius IX making it directly responsible to Rome. Challenged, Meskedra produced the original Charter.

BBB changed tack, and discovered, or said he discovered, a document said to have been signed by the first Abbot confirming that the property belonged to the Diocese of Galway. This posed a problem for Meskedra. The deeds were held by the bank. With Lurglurg's help, he looked through old dust covered trunks stored in the basement and long forgotten. It took days, but eventually he found what he wanted, a receipt made out to Abbot Jose for five thousand pounds plus fifty pounds costs from the firm of O'Higgins, solicitors, Eyre Square, Galway dated 21 October 1927. This clearly specified the amount as the purchase price of Turla Abbey.

Ulick and Ozzy attended the Circuit Court in Galway where Ulick's colleague Marty Walsh was defending the Order against the bishop's efforts to obtain possession of the Abbey. Ulick knew that BBB posed as a kind and saintly churchman to those who knew him not; there weren't many of those around Galway.

The case was heard by Judge Ned Ivers, an elderly, stern, but very fair lawman who didn't mince his words. Ulick and Ozzy sat quietly at the back of the court quite near the august bishop while his solicitor, Gus Silke, handed the document to the Judge, and asked for a possession order. Ulick had reason to believe the Judge wasn't an admirer of the said Bishop.

The judge turned to Marty Walsh to hear his defence.

'Your honour, we can prove the order bought this property with their own money. It's their property. I accept that Brother Jose may have signed this document, but if he did, he did so under false pretences. He had no English; he couldn't know what he was signing, if indeed, he signed anything.'

Gus Silke rose. 'I object, Your Honour, it is inconceivable that a Bishop of the Roman Catholic Church would participate in such a deceit.'

The judge remarked dryly, 'Is it? Who witnessed the signature?'

'The bishop's secretary of the day.'

'Do you propose to call him?'

'No, your honour, he has long since passed to his eternal reward.'

'I see,' but he didn't sound very impressed.

Marty Walsh knew Judge Ivers well enough to know he was having difficulty refusing this order.

He rose. 'Your Honour, I would like to call Patrick McDermott before you decide this matter.'

Gus Silke rose. 'I object, Your Honour, Mr McDermott can have no interest in this application.'

The judge permitted himself a thin smile.

'Wouldn't that be for me to decide, Mr Silke? We'll hear what Mr McDermott has to say.'

Pat McDermott, manager of the Lynch Bank was duly sworn in and took his place on the stand.

Marty Walsh rose. 'Mr McDermott, will you tell the Court what interest you have in this matter.'

Pat McDermott was a small, thin middle aged man with a very sharp mind and a dry sense of humour. He and the Judge played golf together every week, but that would have no bearing on the matter in hand. He had no time for BBB.

'Your Honour, my Bank holds a mortgage on this property. Should you decide to accept this application, we would have to seek immediate repayment in full, or possession of the entire estate.'

Ulick noticed the sudden interest on the part of BBB. He leaned forward frowning. The Bank manager was the only one who noted the judge's favourable reaction to his comments.

'You would not be prepared to transfer the mortgage to the Bishop?'

'No, your honour.'

'It seems you lack confidence in the diocese?'

Pat McDermott smiled and merely nodded.

The judge turned to the Bishop's advocate.

'Mr Silke, do you wish to cross examine the witness?'

'Yes, your honour.'

He looked sternly at the manager.

'Mr McDermott, how much does the order owe your Bank?'

'I haven't got today's balance but it's certainly in excess of five million.'

Silke unhappily. 'That's near enough.' He turned to the judge.

'Your honour, may I consult with my client?'

'Certainly, Mr Silke, we'll break for five minutes.'

After a lively and sometimes acrimonious discussion between BBB and his solicitor, the Court resumed.

Mr Silke rose. 'Your honour, my client would like to consider this matter in greater detail. Accordingly I would ask that you adjourn for a month.'

The judge looked at Marty Walsh who nodded agreement.

'Very well, we'll adjourn for one month. This court is now adjourned.'

Ulick and Ozzy met Meskedra when he emerged from the court with a jubilant Lurglurg.

'You won the day, Meskedra, but BBB is far from beaten.'

'No one knows that better than I do.' He lowered his voice.

'I may be able to help with your battle against the big Count. I am a man of many talents.'

Ulick shook his head sagely. 'Now that, I do believe. Will you meet me in Paulo's tonight, if that is permitted by the rules of the order?'

He grinned. 'I'll be there. We are a very Christian order.'

'You might even join us for a pint of the hard stuff?'

He grinned. 'Certainly not: I only drink the finest brandy.'

He rejoined Lurglurg and departed.

Ulick turned to Ozzy smiling. 'Now there's a brand of Christianity I could take to. And they do say he's an even bigger hammer man than BBB!'

***

Ulick was ending his discussions with Meskedra when Frank arrived; he ordered two pints and a brandy for the man of the cloth.

'Frank' he began, 'Abbot Meskedra has been telling me about his Poitin service. I think we could apply that idea to our farming business that was.'

Frank had heard so many different stories about Meskedra that he viewed him with some scepticism.

'I'm all for anything that will stop our farmers sitting around all day scratching their arses.'

'I'll let Meskedra tell you about it.'

The good abbot put down his glass.

'The farmers are not allowed to grow crops commercially; they're paid well to sit around, as you say. It's bad for their morale; it's making them soft and useless; they're drinking too much; it's even bad for their spirituality.'

Ulick grunted amiably. 'It's not like you to be talking about the spirit.'

He grinned. 'I know, I think the job is getting to me. Anyway, your farmers are entitled to grow as much produce as they wish for their own use but they're not allowed to sell it. My suggestion is that they devise an offerings system - like we have in Turla. The USE cannot object to it; the proceeds would be tax free to them; and your imports would reduce.'

Frank scratched his head. 'Be God, that's a great idea.'

***

Dan strutted around the underground silo while preparations to launch twenty missiles were completed. None of the operators looked very pleased. Far above them, the gigantic roof parted to reveal a clear moonlit sky. The countdown continued; with one minute go the afterburners were lit. The co-ordinates were checked carefully. The monotonous voice continued 10-9-8-7-6-5-4-3-2-1 LAUNCH.

Dan watched while the rockets lifted off and disappeared into the night sky. The roof above closed; the operators tracked the progress of the missiles on radar. The Commander stood behind one of the operators.

'Where are they now?'

'Crossing North of Paris, sir.'

'Estimated time of attack?'

'Fifteen minutes, sir.'

'Estimated casualties?'

'Probably fifty thousand.'

Dan shook his little fist up at them. 'Bad men, I fix ya.'

Suddenly, alarm bells started screaming throughout the command area.

'What the hell is wrong?' The Commander demanded angrily.

'The missiles are turning south on a new course.'

The rest of the staff gathered around the command computer.

'Do something,' the Commander screamed.

He punched in some instructions. 'It's no good, they're not responding.'

'Where are they headed now?'

He checked the radar again. 'On a course that will take them towards Lake Constance.'

'Jeesus, that's where the Count has his palace, hit the self destruct button.'

The missiles would explode harmlessly in mid air.

The operator sounded panicky. 'It's not responding. We've lost all control.'

'Are they still on the same heading?'

'Yes, sir.'

'Can we put up fighters to shoot them down?'

'No, sir, they're designed to evade fighters. We have to issue a warning.'

The Commander intervened. 'No, no warning.'

'But they're heading towards Friedrick's Haven. We have to warn the Count.'

'No, no warning.'

'Commander, I'm going to warn him. He can move his family and staff to the fallout shelter under the castle.'

Reluctantly, the Commander gave in but before Rolf could pick up the phone the operator announced.

'They're changing course again.'

Then he rose screaming. 'They're coming directly for us. I'm getting out of here.'

The main alarm started to wail - followed by a rush towards the lifts. The loudspeakers announced. "General evacuation – 10 minutes and counting."

Dan danced around clapping his hands. What a sight! He was in the car park at ground level when the fearful evacuees raced to their cars, revved up and, with screaming tyres, drove recklessly up the autobahn towards higher ground some five kilometres away. Dan sat in the last jeep, still clapping his little hands, as he was bumped around unceremoniously. The cavalcade stopped on the high ground. All eyes turned to the silo below.

Then, the awesome, high pitched screams when the missiles approached at a height of 500 feet. Dan pointed his index finger at them. They stopped above the silo. Some of the women started to cry while everyone crouched down fearfully behind the jeeps and cars.

'What the hell is going on?' the Commander demanded.

'They're just sitting there. No one is going to believe this.'

Dan pointed again; the rockets moved swiftly towards the west, their turbines screaming louder than ever when they passed above the petrified silo people. Time to go.

Surrounded by his famous paintings, not that he ever looked at them; the big Count finished his sumptuous dinner, lit a cigar and sipped his brandy. He always dined alone. His expression was relaxed, almost benign while he awaited confirmation that Galway had been destroyed. Then, he would send his fleet to take charge of the Aran and Achill refineries. He was not aware that Dan was sitting on the other end of the long mahogany table.

I'll fix you, ya big bully.

Suddenly, the castle was rocked by the thunderous noise of twenty missiles blasting their way through the night air above. The Count leapt up, spilling his brandy, his face white in terror and raced out to the balcony. Dan joined him, and stood up on the parapet. He pointed his index finger. The missiles, racing out across the lake, made a u turn and headed back towards the castle. This was too much for the Count's paranoia.

'They're coming for me: Got in Himmel save me.'

He staggered into the room and darted under the table. His collie dog, resting quietly there, got up and raced out of the room.

Dan watched as the missiles swished by again completed another u turn and headed back towards the castle. He pointed again. The missiles slowed down and assembled in a circle above the front lawn. Very slowly, they sank to earth and sat vertically on the lawn. All became silent.

When the staff arrived Dan strolled into the dining room. The big Count crawled from under the table. The butler looked distinctly disappointed to see that his master was still alive. Tentatively at first, the Count approached the door to the balcony. He relaxed visibly when he saw the silent missiles.

Dan allowed him to hear him laugh derisively.

'Do you hear that?' he demanded of his butler.

'I don't hear anything, sire.'

'Get me the Commander.'

The big Count paused. Did he hear someone laugh? Or was it that little voice in his head again?

***

The following morning's TV news carried live pictures of the missiles standing on the Count's lawn; it wasn't long before the full story emerged.

Ulick went on HBTV two hours later.

'Fellow citizens, last night, we deflected missiles targeted at Galway by the big Count. In a gesture of humanity, we refrained from destroying the Count's castle with his own missiles.

I am warning you now, Count Otto. Any further such attacks, and we will launch our missiles without warning.' He paused.

'I do agree with the Count on one thing. It is unacceptable that weapons of mass destruction be under the control of a lunatic.'

***

The near empty morning flight from New York touched down at Galway International. Gone were the days when this flight was full of cheerful American tourists. There was one American, a fit looking man with swarthy features, greying hair and cool blue eyes, wearing blue jeans and a heavy red shirt; but Nick Forde wasn't a tourist. An anonymous phone call to Langley gave his superiors the opportunity they wanted; to get rid of him for a while. Nick knew that but it suited him to go along with it.

Nearly fifty now, Nick Forde had been the CIA senior operative in the Middle East. He saw the coming together of the Arab nations and warned his superiors, several times, long before it occurred. But his immediate superior, John Wallace refused to believe him until it was far too late do anything about it. He scrapped Nick's reports and, when the White House came looking for his head, calmly insisted he never received any warnings.

Nick might have had a bad accident if Wallace could be sure that copies of the reports didn't exist. A break in at Nick's apartment in Jerusalem failed to find copies. They daren't sack him, or force him to retire, in case he went public; so they kept him hanging around doing odd jobs while they tried to figure out what to do with him.

He had been with the firm for nearly thirty years, served in many parts of the world and had the reputation of being a thoroughly reliable operative. Thankfully, his dear wife Millie didn't live to witness his shafting. She died two years earlier; their only son, Edward, was a successful computer programmer in San Francisco.

Nick longed to retire to the little town of High Falls on the Colorado River where he spent many happy vacations with Millie. There he could sit back, sip his Jack Daniels, let the world go by and pursue his love of fishing.

He hired a taxi at the airport to take him to Turla Lodge Hotel in Maam Valley. The anonymous phone caller said the Hibernian Government had a missile silo somewhere near the hotel. He knew it was a wild goose chase, but he liked this part of Ireland, and it would give him time to think about the future.

***

Meskedra was sitting in his favourite armchair in reception - sipping his brandy - looking out on the car park and lake beyond. Lurglurg was at the desk, not that there was any activity as occupancy was down to sixty guests, mostly from Dublin. Unknown to both of them, Dan was sitting nearby. Meskedra had promised to help Ulick convince the Americans that they really had missiles; a laudable idea, but Dan. just didn't trust the affable churchman.

A taxi pulled up outside; Nick Forde alighted; took his bag and entered reception. He stopped in his tracks when he saw Meskedra. His expression said "Where have I seen this guy before?"

Meskedra frowned, but made a point of meeting the new guest.

'Welcome to Turla Lodge Hotel sir.'

'Nice place you got here. How is the fishing?'

'It's good this time of year. Can we offer you a nice room overlooking the lake?'

'That will be fine. The name is Nick Forde, from New York.'

Meskedra looked at Lurglurg. 'I hope you have a pleasant stay, Mr Forde. Brother Lurglurg will take care of you.'

In a puzzled state of mind, he left reception and returned to his apartment. If he was puzzled, Dan was baffled. What is going on here?

'Is that the Boss?' Nick enquired.

'Yes, sir.'

'Is it not unusual to have an order of monks run a hotel?'

He eyes opened wide in admiration when one of the attractive waitresses walked by.

Lurglurg frowned. 'As the Abbot often says, sir "Did not our Lord himself feed the hungry?"

He liked it. 'How long has the abbot been here?'

'About six years, sir. I'll show you to your room.'

***

Dan found Meskedra sitting before his computer screen. He had thrown off his habit, and looked quite trendy in a white shirt over grey slacks. Dan got up on a chair to get a better look at the screen; it showed a picture of a modern missile and some very strange figures. Meskedra smiled to himself as he pushed the print button and took another sip from his glass. But he was puzzled. After a carefully placed phone call, through Iceland, he expected a visit from the CIA but this fellow Nick Forde? He was sure he had seen him before: but where? When the printer stopped he exited the Internet: he had just hacked into one of the most secure computers in the world and successfully covered his tracks.

Dan stood on the chair, watching him. I do not trust you, holy man.

***

Meskedra made a point of meeting Nick Forde at breakfast.

'Enjoying your stay, sir?'

'Yes, everything is fine. By the way, what should I call you?'

'Brother Meskedra is the name.'

Dan could see they were fencing with one another.

'I hear, Meskedra, you have a booze distillery here. Can I see it?'

'Of course. I'll show you after breakfast.'

'Do I have to put something in the offerings box?'

'No, it's included in your room rate.'

When they entered the newly installed lift, and went down two floors, Dan accompanied them. Nick became very interested in the Poitin distillery. Meskedra showed him how it worked, and presented him with a bottle of the PD brand. In an offhand manner, Nick enquired about the tunnel at the back of the distillery; this was just what Meskedra wanted.

'Oh, that! It runs under the mountain where silver was mined long ago.'

'Does it come out the other side?'

He appeared to hesitate. 'I'm not sure; I've never dared venture that far.'

Everyone satisfied, they returned to the hotel, where Nick ordered a taxi to take him to Conna.

***

The big Count conducted affairs of state from his study overlooking the lake. Every morning, after his customary joust in the gymnasium, he walked his two Labradors through his tree lined gardens. When not too preoccupied with planning the future history of the world, he would pause to look across at the island of Mainau where his unfortunate brother languished. Their last encounter became very violent; Gunter even threatened to shoot him; best not go there again.

He was angry when he returned to the study to greet the Admiral of the USE Fleet, Admiral Jose Miguel Antonio Sebastian, who was sweating profusely, having already been warned about the Count's short fuse. A native of Madrid, grey haired and overweight, he looked the part in his new blue uniform with his chest covered in medals. Apart from manoeuvres and war games, he had never seen live action in his life but the medals looked impressive. Not knowing what to do he bowed before his master and then saluted; the Count, with barely a glance at him, took his place behind the large mahogany desk. Dan stood by the window watching them.

'Admiral,' he bellowed, 'how soon can you have the fleet ready to sail?'

He paused to think about it.

'Quickly, man I'm in a hurry.'

'Ah, a month, sir.'

'Too long. I want you to be ready to sail in ten days.'

The admiral sincerely hoped they weren't going to invade America.

He coughed. 'If I sail without the aircraft carriers, I can be ready in two weeks.'

'Ten days, that's all you've got.'

'May I enquire, sir, where will we be going?'

'To this damned place called,' he rooted around on his desk, 'Hibernia. You will have fifty thousand troops under the command of General Conti. Your mission will be to capture,' again he rooted around, 'A city called Galway and take control of my oil refineries. Can you do it?'

'Of course, sir, I'll assemble the fleet off Cadiz.'

He dismissed him. 'Send in Williams.'

Dan raised his little fist at him. I fix you, ya big bully.

Commander Bendes was furious when he heard the Count was giving orders directly to his subordinates that should come through him. He cooled down a bit when he heard the details; this was an operation he would not have agreed to.

***

Following the near collapse of the Community, the Count replaced most of the senior administrators. He appointed George Williams as his Senior Political adviser, not that he took advice from anyone but he still required the structure to carry out his orders. George Williams was the UK representative on the council of ministers and, for the past ten years, served in Brussels as co-ordinator in long term planning. A weedy, boffin type little man of forty one, he got on well with his master - whom he admired - and enjoyed the heady atmosphere of power. He could thank his enemies in Brussels for this appointment; they just wanted to get rid of him; now, he would take care of them at his leisure.

The Count trusted him: of that he was sure, and to a degree, he was right. The Count trusted him to do his dirty work. That suited him. The Count wouldn't always be god. Afterwards a safe pair of hands would be necessary; who better than someone with his vast experience?

The Count was drumming the desk impatiently with his fingers when his assistant joined him.

'What news from America, Williams?' He never called him by his Christian name.

'We have a stand-off in the Middle East, sire. The American sixth Fleet is anchored off the coast of Israel. It's a very delicate situation.'

'What about the oil?'

'The new Turkish regime won't resume shipments of oil until Israel agrees to join the confederation.'

'That will never happen. Now, all we have to do is recover my refineries off that damned place called, what the hell is it?'

'Hibernia, sir.'

He paused. 'Have you checked up on my brother recently?'

'Yes, sir. I was over there last week. They have to keep him mildly sedated most of the time. He's suffering from all kinds of hallucinations.'

'Poor fellow. Would it not be better to let him escape this dreadful world?'

'I'm sure it would, sir, but it would need to appear to be from natural causes.'

He grunted. 'I'll think about it. Now, what about those rockets that fellow Joyc says he has?'

'Just talk, sire.'

'Rubbish. I know they exist. We have to find out where they are and send in the bombers.'

***

Nick Forde waited until the house settled down for the night. Then, armed with his camera, torch and Magnum he slipped out of his room and made his way downstairs; he daren't use the lift. He, eventually, found the stairs down to the distillery. This was easier than he expected, but he was unaware he was accompanied by a smiling Dan. He stopped briefly at the distillery. There was complete silence apart from the rhythmic hissing sound of the wash. Checking his bearings, he selected the tunnel running directly under the mountain and proceeded slowly. Ignoring the electric light switches, he used his powerful torch. Dan cantered along quietly behind.

On they went for quite some time. The rough walls were covered with cob webs, the air dank and stale. Nick, thinking he was wasting his time, turned back.

He suddenly spotted a modern recessed steel door he hadn't noticed before. Dan smiled as Nick opened the door, to reveal a short corridor leading to an elevator. He entered; it had only two buttons; he pushed the lower one and the lift descended quickly. It stopped eventually. He stepped out, and looked around cautiously; he was in a modern, gigantic missile silo. There was no one in sight. All he could hear was the noise of sophisticated ventilation and temperature control systems. He whistled under his breath: this was some operation.

Taking out his camera he took photos of the rows of missiles in launch position. He peered up into darkness; there had to be a false roof up there somewhere for launching. The control unit must be on a different level.

Dan cantered around after him; the little man looked quite pleased with himself. Satisfied that he had all he needed, Nick took the lift to the surface and retraced his steps back to the hotel. He smiled to himself as he prepared for bed. There were all kinds of possibilities here.

Dan looked in on Meskedra who was busily putting the finishing touches to his drawings. He was intrigued by this unusual man of the cloth. Once a year, Meskedra travelled to London to meet someone in secret; an older man he called "uncle" but from the time he left Dublin until he returned he was dressed like an aristocrat and called himself Simon Longfellow. Dan found this all very confusing. I will be watching you, brother Meskedra, or whoever you are. You are up to no good. I fix ya.

In the morning, Nick Forde ordered a taxi to take him to the airport, and checked out of the hotel.

***

In the Oval Office in the White House in Washington President Elaine Byrne consulted her Secretary of State, Chris Vance. She was worried: with good reason. An international crisis was brewing; that in itself wasn't so unusual but this time her options were very limited. The really worrying part: she was afraid of being forced into a situation where the only viable option would involve major conflict.

Nearly 51 now, still a very attractive woman with long blonde hair, strong features and clear blue eyes, she wore a dark business suit with a white blouse: in the informality of the Oval Office she discarded the jacket. Brought up in a political family in New York, she studied

Law and Economics at Columbia University with her sights firmly set on a political career. Her father served two terms in the United States Senate and was nominated once for vice President.

She began her career as an economics lecturer in Harvard before running, on the Democratic ticket, for a Senate seat in New York. It had been a long, slow and sometimes frustrating climb. She was finally elected Governor of New York State, having failed to get the nomination on two previous occasions. This put her under enormous pressure to do her job, keep her marriage going, and bring up her son. In the end, her husband, a leading New York lawyer divorced her. They remained good friends. He remarried a year later. She did not form any lasting relationships after that; her son, John was now serving in the US Navy.

After two terms in opposition, the Democrats were determined to find a candidate who would bring them the White House. Their desperation, and her obvious ability, got her a nomination she would not otherwise be considered for. She won, and set about implementing her policies. Lacking a majority in both Houses of the Congress made this a mammoth task, but she persevered and achieved considerable success in developing her social and economic programme. Her re election prospects were now seriously threatened by the Middle East crisis. The price of oil had already tripled.

Chris Vance was the Law Professor in Harvard when Elaine Byrne lectured there. They became good friends; he was ten years her senior. Tall and handsome, with a tinge of grey and shrewd hazel eyes he had what she needed most: integrity. She was friendly with his third wife, Sandra and often visited their summer home at Cape Cod. He accepted the position of Secretary of State and became her most trusted ally and confidante in the Government. He waited calmly for her to commence.

'What do you think, Chris? Will the Count invade Hibernia?'

'He keeps talking about the threat Joyc poses to world peace with his weapons of mass destruction. Insists he'll act. Turned down our suggestion of weapons inspectors out of hand.' He paused. 'If he does invade we're in real trouble.'

'Why do you say that?'

'We've committed the Sixth Fleet to remaining in the Mediterranean to act as a deterrent to Turkey.'

'Have we any reserves?'

'We have two subs in the Gulf, but they couldn't stop a full scale attack. Your predecessor scrapped most of the navy in favour of missiles.'

'We have to have oil from Aran, Chris. Will you contact President Joyc? We will pay whatever price he asks.'

He was silent for a moment.

'What about the advanced weapons Joyc says he has?'

'I've asked the CIA to look into it. After letting us be caught flat footed in the Middle East, maybe the fools will do better this time.'

'I wouldn't count on it. Do you think I should travel to Friedrick's Haven and try to talk sense to the Count?'

'It's worth a try, I suppose.' She paused. 'Now I have to convene a meeting of the Joint Chiefs and hear what they have to say.'

***

Admiral Sebastian stood on the deck of his flagship, The United States of Europe - anchored off Cadiz - and looked about him proudly. Now, at last, his opportunity for glory; a great venture recorded for posterity on live TV. Afterwards, he could look forward to a political career; and maybe, one day, succeed the great Count. As soon as his enormous fleet sailed, he would immerse himself in the naval manuals borrowed from the marine college in Athens.

The bay was cluttered with battleships, cruisers, troopships and car ferries, now being used to transport tanks. In the docks, he could see large numbers of troops lining up. Most of the provisions were already on board. He looked at his watch; everything was going according to plan; his great armada would sail at midnight.

Dan was very upset and angry at the prospect of Galway being invaded by such bad people. What could he do? He wandered through the operations room, watched the computer operators studying weather charts and plotting a course for Galway. He would have to think of something. Shaking his little fist at them he departed.

***

Ulick was joined by Ozzy in Paulo's; a very agitated Frank arrived a few minutes later. Ulick ordered three pints.

'Have you heard the news, Ulick?' Frank demanded.

'No.'

'I just heard from a friend who has an Irish pub in Cadiz. The big Count is going to invade us.'

'I've talked with Chris Vance in Washington. He's going to see the Count to warn him that any such action would be treated by the US as an act of war.'

'That won't stop the big Count, Ulick. He has already told President Byrne to but out.'

***

Abbot Meskedra sat in his usual armchair, sipping his brandy. A taxi pulled up outside and a tall, quite stunning looking, blonde alighted. She looked around at the beauty of her surroundings and, eventually her gaze fell on Meskedra. He sat up in his chair; put down his glass. They recognised each other immediately. He leapt up and left reception in such haste that Lurglurg, who was looking after the desk, gazed after him in surprise; he had never seen the boss move so fast. The lady entered and approached the desk, accompanied by the taxi driver carrying her bag. She looked around for Meskedra with a little smile on her face, while she took her bag and paid the driver.

'May I have a room please?' she inquired. 'One overlooking the lake.'

'Certainly madam, please sign the register.'

As she did so, she inquired. 'Who is that monk I saw just now?'

'He's the Boss, I mean Brother Meskedra the Abbot of the Fathers of the Brothers.'

She tried to get her head around that mouthful.

'Has he been here long?'

'About six years, let me show you to your room, madam.'

Meskedra, observed by Dan, poured himself a large brandy, in what he called his den. Paulette here, I can't believe it. What do I do now? She is so beautiful. Seven, no, eight years since we parted in Paris. Now, fate has brought her to Turla Lodge.

In her room, overlooking the lake, Paulette's emotions were in danger of running riot. Andre, my beloved Andre, a monk? I don't believe it. Stop behaving like a bashful schoolgirl, you're here on business. It's so exciting. I'm sure he recognised me. Changing her designer pale cream suit for a clinging light beige dress, she paid particular attention to her appearance. Then, taking a book, she left the hotel and sat in the shade of an old oak tree by the lake. She pretended to read, but her mind was in a state of confusion.

She watched Meskedra leave the hotel, and approach quietly from behind. She turned and looked up at him with a mocking smile.

'This is the last place I expected to find you, Andre.'

He loved that smile. He sat down beside her.

'You are as beautiful as ever, dear Paulette; I'm so happy to see you again. Mama had a stroke. I had to leave Paris at a moment's notice. When I rang the hotel you had checked out.'

'You haven't changed; just as big a flatterer as ever, but Andre in a monk's robes; I just don't believe it.'

'After Mama died I sold the chateau and vineyard - went to America, finished up in Rio. There, I saw the light.'

'You joined a very enlightened order. Lurglurg, the unsmiling one, has been telling me about your variable vows.'

'They are excellent character builders. You cannot be a saint without first being a sinner.'

'So only sinners go to Heaven?'

'Unfortunately, no but the good Lord loves the sinner. He must find the holy Joe's and holy Mary's depressingly boring.'

'But variable vows?'

He grinned. 'To go without any of life's little pleasures, permanently, is painful - only for a time: it becomes extremely painful when you vary your abstinence. Each time you give up a pleasure, even for a short time, it becomes ever more painful, and tests your strength of character.'

'Your logic is impeccable.' She looked around her. 'It's so peaceful here.'

'It won't be if the Count invades.'

She shook her head again. 'Andre a monk, I still can't believe it.'

'I sometimes wonder myself. You won't let on?'

'Your secret is safe with me.'

'Will you join me for dinner tonight?'

'I would love to, but is that allowed?'

'Of course, we are a very Christian order.'

He observed Nick Forde getting out of a taxi and entering the hotel.

'I'll wear my most alluring dress.'

'Do, Lurglurg always says, the Lord wouldn't have made woman so beautiful if he didn't want man to be tempted.'

She liked it.

'That's a new slant on an old theory. So I could be giving scandal.'

'No, no, we don't have scandal in this order; we leave that to the secular clergy.'

***

Dinner was a sumptuous banquet, presented by a very surprised Brother Mungo, a master chef with more than a passing love for PD. He had never seen the Boss entertain a lady before; neither had Nick Forde, nor a very bemused Dan. Nick was wondering where the beautiful blonde fitted in: he was also wondering where the hell he had seen this guy before. Meskedra, who was quietly observing him, was wondering where the hell he had seen Nick Forde before.

After a main course of salmon followed by a bottle of Chilean white, Paulette looked around the half empty room.

'This hotel can't be making money?'

'It used to be very profitable. This time of year the house would normally be full of Americans. But along comes the political crisis; no Americans; no money; no smiling Bank manager.'

'Can't you do anything?'

'Hope and pray it doesn't last too long.'

She leaned across and put her hand on his. 'Andre, let me help.'

'I couldn't do that.'

She lowered her voice. 'Andre, if I could find a way to help, would it bother your conscience if it wasn't strictly above board?'

'I couldn't let you do that; you might get into trouble.'

She smiled. 'It's good of you to be concerned about me. I was sent here to buy the plans of the secret weapon your President talks about.'

He laughed. 'It's one of the fairy tales of Hibernia. Ulick is bluffing.'

She lowered her voice again. 'No, he's not. I've seen the photos. I'll show them to you later.'

This, he didn't understand but he kept a straight face. Dan understood.

'What photos?'

'The pictures taken by a CIA man who was over here.'

'How would your principles get such information from the CIA?'

'They bought them from the CIA man concerned. Everyone has his price these days.'

'So why not buy the plans from the CIA man?'

'He apparently hasn't got them yet; and it's possible he won't get them. My principles will pay you five million dollars.' She paused. 'Andre, I will gladly donate that sum to your order.'

He was trying to get his head around this; there was something going on he didn't know about, but that wasn't important right now. Nick Forde was in business for himself: now, that was interesting.

'Paulette, it would be immoral to sell those plans.'

She smiled - how he loved that smile. 'If I don't get them someone else will. It can hardly be immoral to help your brothers.'

He appeared to consider it.

'It would certainly take a load off my mind.'

'Please let me do this for you. Then I'll give up spying.' She paused. 'Are you disappointed in me?'

He grinned mockingly. 'And all that time in Paris you never hinted.'

'How could I? A French gentleman doesn't associate with a con artist busily selling genuine, Picasso fakes.'

He smiled, he was really enjoying this. 'I could almost approve of selling fakes to greedy collectors. It's entirely consistent with my variable vow of honesty.'

'I'm so relieved.' She looked at her watch. 'It's time any self respecting con artist retired.'

Much to Lurglurg's approval, he kissed her hand gallantly and she departed.

***

Dan stood beside Admiral Sebastian while he briefed his computer operators. In twenty minutes, the mighty fleet would sail from Cadiz. Captain Erwin Harpzig watched with interest.

Erwin Harpzig's parents immigrated to the Unites States after the war. His father was a nuclear physicist. Erwin wasn't interested in the academic life; he joined the American navy at eighteen and operated out of San Diego where he lived with the first of his three wives. He was promoted to First Officer on the USS Washington before the administration decided to scrap most of the navy.

At fifty, he joined the new USE navy where he was appointed Captain of the USE flagship. His third wife Emma lived with him in Cadiz. They were visited frequently by his two daughters from his previous marriages. A thoroughly professional and highly experienced officer, he had little time for what he called "armchair admirals" like Sebastian.

The Admiral continued. 'Set a course to a rendezvous point one hundred kilometres due West of Aran. We will take Galway first. It will then be a simple operation to take control of the refinery on Aran before moving on to Achill.'

Captain Harpzig inquired. 'Do you want to maintain radio silence?'

'Yes, Captain.'

'What about the TV crews?'

'They can take all the shots they like while we are at sea, but only the surrender of Galway will go out live.'

'Admiral, are we expecting any resistance?'

He turned to the General Luigi Conti. 'What do you think?'

'Our intelligence sources say this will be what you call a duck shoot.'

'What about the missiles they claim to have?'

'They won't be a problem. We are fully equipped with anti missile missiles.'

The admiral looked at his watch. 'That's fine.' He tapped one of the operators on the shoulder. 'Jacques, make sure the fleet stays in formation, and let me know when I can expect to be joined by the aircraft carriers, "Normandy" and "Venice."

'Yes, sir.'

The Admiral went to his cabin, locked the door firmly behind him and took took a book entitled "Strategies of naval warfare" from his briefcase and began to read.

General Luigi Conti, thirty four, handsome and flamboyant, a native of Modena, trained at the military college in Milan but he had no experience of real warfare. The fact that his uncle was the Italian Premier had everything to do with his getting this appointment. A playboy, with a large number of female friends, he didn't see any reason why he shouldn't continue his agreeable style of living.

Dan waved his little fist at them. Bad men, I fix the lot of you; but he had no idea how this could be achieved.

***

Meskedra knew Nick Forde would come to see him; sure enough, there was a tap on his apartment door just before midnight. He invited him in and offered him a brandy that he gratefully accepted.

'Take a seat, Mr Forde.'

He sipped the brandy. 'Call me Nick. This brandy is a lot kinder than your PD brand.'

He smiled. He didn't know why, but he liked this guy.

'CIA?'

'You got it.' He paused, shaking his head. 'Damned if I can place it, but I've seen you somewhere before.'

Meskedra smiled agreeably. 'Perhaps, I was a jack of all trades before I joined the Order.'

'Anyway, to business. I want the blueprints of Joyc's missiles.'

This was met with a wide grin. 'Come again.'

He produced a bundle of photos, and handed them over. 'Don't bullshit me. Nothing goes on around here without you knowing about it.'

They were the same photos that Paulette showed him. Ulick's friends must be up to their tricks again. Dan, sitting in his comfortable armchair nodded agreement. Meskedra examined the pictures and handed them back.

Nick continued. 'Don't get me wrong. My people will pay well for the blueprints; I have a score to settle with those bastards. You could use some money for this hotel. You're living off PD or PPS although I'm damned if I can tell the difference: apart from the cost.'

He appeared to ponder the idea.

'We are certainly strapped for cash. Five million dollars would help.'

Nick finished his drink and stood up. 'That's damn good brandy. I'll be back in three days with the money; have the blueprints ready.'

They shook hands, Meskedra held the door to let his guest depart. Nick stopped on the doorstep. 'It just keeps bugging me. I know I've seen you somewhere before: sure as hell you weren't dressed as a monk.'

***

Ulick met Frank and Ozzy in Paulo's after a short TV appearance in which he made it clear the people of Hibernia would defend themselves against all invaders. If necessary, he would use his secret Paddyrockets. He called on all members of the USE to come to their assistance and get rid of the Big Count before he plunged the entire world into chaos.

Paulo put three pints before them. 'Will it do any good, Ulick?' he asked in worried tones.

'We have to wait and see. President Byrne will be making a TV address in two hours time warning the big Count that her Government will resist any attack on our country.'

Paulo looked relieved. 'We're safe then. The big count wouldn't dare take on America.'

Ulick shook his head. 'No, we're only getting two nuclear subs. That won't be nearly enough if our information is correct.'

'Where are they now?'

'Somewhere west of Jersey the last we heard.'

Frank reacted angrily. 'There must be something we can do?'

Paulo responded. 'Couldn't we put together an army of volunteers?'

Ulick shook his head. 'No, we would be in more danger from them than the enemy. I've sent Moxy to see the other USE leaders. They can't be too happy with this situation.'

'So what do we do then?' Frank demanded.

'We may have to let them in; then resort to guerrilla warfare. We'll make it hot for them.'

Ozzy sipped his drink, looking extremely depressed.

***

Meskedra met Paulette in reception when she checked out; he carried her bag to the waiting taxi while Lurglurg hovered around attentively. Dressed in a clinging beige dress, he thought she looked absolutely lovely. Perhaps if things had been different, he thought wistfully, but they're not. She smiled; bravely conscious they might not meet again.

'Andre, I'll be back with the money as soon as I can.'

'I will count the days until you return.'

'Can I kiss you goodbye?'

'I think Lurglurg would be scandalised.'

'I don't think he would.' She kissed him lightly on the cheek. 'Adieu Andre, my love.'

Lurglurg looked quite pleased.

She got into the taxi quickly.

As it pulled away, Lurglurg approached him.

'Will she be coming back, Boss?'

'I truly don't know.'

***

In the Atlantic, a great storm blew in from the Caribbean with waves up to fifty feet high, scattering the fleet over a wide area. The Admiral sat in his big leather bound chair on the bridge while the automated steering system fought to keep the ship steady into the mounting waves. They would just have to sit it out. Captain Herzog handed him the latest weather report. Growling in disgust, he handed it back. Gales would continue for another two days. Heaving his bulk out of the chair he decided to go below to study his manuals.

Dan was very vexed when he arrived on the bridge - he began to feel queasy with the deck heaving under his feet. He went immediately to the operations room and stood behind the unhappy looking computer operators. How could he stop these bad people from destroying his beloved Galway? When his stomach began to rumble, he departed hastily.

***

Nick Forde returned to Turla, carrying a large holdall, still looking like an out of work plumber. Lurglurg escorted him to Meskedra's apartment. He put the bag on the table. Meskedra didn't pass any heed of it.

'Aren't you going to count it?'

'No, I trust you.'

Going to his desk, he extracted a thick folder and handed it over. Nick inspected it briefly. Dan watched with interest.

'I finally figured it out,' Nick looked at him shrewdly. 'It was Rio, wasn't it?'

He smiled and nodded.

'According to the official record you're dead. You don't have to worry about me.'

'Have you sorted out your masters yet?'

He smiled. 'Yes, but the stupid bastards don't know it. They paid fifteen million for the blueprints; five for you and ten for me. I can afford to retire now.'

'You're nearly as good as I used to be.'

'No, not even in the same class. Is it true you sold sand to Oilcorp?'

'Yes, but they thought there was oil under it.'

Nick suddenly had a thought. 'You wouldn't think of selling this lot to anyone else, would you?'

'Good Heavens, no. What do you think I am?'

He grinned. 'I know what you are.' He put out his hand. 'It's been a pleasure doing business with you. Now I've got a plane to catch.'

'Go in peace and enjoy your retirement.'

'I'll see myself out.'

After Nick departed, Meskedra carried the bag down to reception.
'Lurglurg, will you get me a taxi. I have to go into Galway.'

Arriving at the Lynch Bank, he told the taxi to wait. He walked briskly into the bank. Dan cantered along behind him. Meskedra went to the safe deposit vault, opened his box and placed the holdall in it. Dan stood there, scratching his head. The money was in the bank but was it in the bank?

He was even more puzzled when Meskedra went to a nearby phone box, dialled a number, and then spoke in a different accent.

'Is that Bishop Brennan? Never mind who I am. I just want to let you know that crowd in Turla Lodge have paid off the bank.'

He hung up before he could be questioned, and returned to his taxi.

Dandaboy stood there in the Square trying to figure it out. I'll be watching you Meskedra. I do not trust thee.

***

The Atlantic storm passed on, followed by calm dry weather, much to the relief of the Admiral, who didn't enjoy being at sea even at the best of times. He made his way to the operations room, where the Captain was watching one of the main computer screens. Dan was watching too.

'What's our present position?' he inquired.

'We're one hundred kilometres west of Aran, sir.'

'Have we rounded up the rest of the fleet yet?'

'They're all back on station.'

'Have we a weather forecast for the next three days?'

'High pressure, sir, could be some haze.'

'Good, work out a schedule that will take us into Galway Bay late tomorrow night.'

Dan watched the computer screen for a while. Then he waved his little fist at the Admiral. I fix ya, ya big bully. Plenty haze.

***

Ulick faced the TV camera in a broadcast going out live worldwide; he made no effort to conceal his anger and defiance.

'I am reliably informed that our country is about to be invaded by a massive USE force. We are a peace loving people; we do not want conflict with anyone, but we will, if necessary, defend our rights to the death. For how much longer are you going to put up with this lunatic Count?'

He paused and looked directly at the camera.

'Count, you invade my country at your peril. If you enter our national waters, I will launch our missiles, and send your mighty fleet to the bottom of the Atlantic.

I thank President Byrne for her support at this crucial time. Good people of Hibernia: stay calm. We will prevail.'

***

Leaving Government Buildings, with Frank, Ulick was surprised to find a large crowd waiting for him. They roared their approval; the cheering continued while they got into the waiting car and set out for Conna.

Frank was worried. 'I've just been told the American subs won't be here for another three days.'

'Damn, that will be too late.'

'What are we going to do, Ulick?'

Dan was their only hope, but how could the little man stop a whole bloody fleet?

'We'll just have to hope for a miracle.'

***

In the operations centre the Captain annouced proudly. 'We have entered Galway Bay.'

His main computer operator added. 'In this fog we'll have to reduce speed considerably and rely on radar: in fact, we may have to postpone the attack.'

The Admiral wasn't having it. He turned to General Conti. 'How do you assess the situation?'

The general nodded, pointing to the geographic outline computer screen.

'We will land a small force, spearheaded by tanks, on the Northern and Southern shores. Opposition will be minimal. Galway is on the

Northern side of the bay that terminates eight kilometres further east. Using our Southern command, we will move quickly to round the end of the bay and attack from the east. Our forces on the northern side will attack the city from the West; we will have the enemy in a pincer movement.'

The admiral turned to the Captain. 'Have you deployed our anti missile missiles?'

'Yes, sir.'

'Well then, it's all going according to plan.'

At four in the morning, as dawn approached, the operation commenced. Radar operators checked and rechecked their dials. With Major Duval in charge of the northern landing area, the giant tank carriers eased very slowly towards the shore, hampered by dense fog that showed no sign of lifting. His troops checked their kits anxiously; this would be their first experience of real combat. The TV crews roundly cursed the weather while they checked their equipment, and demanded help in loading it on one of the landing craft.

The atmosphere grew tenser - confusion increased with much loud cursing and swearing as the troops clambered down into the landing crafts. Admiral Sebastian stood on the upper deck listening to the crafts departing into the fog. Was it such a good idea undertaking an amphibious landing in such circumstances? He would have to look up the manual.

An hour later, General Conti rang Major Duval on the radio telephone. His forces should be assembled on land and ready to advance.

'It's the damn visibility, sir. It's going to be very tricky to get near enough the shore to land the tanks.'

The General cursed. 'Why the hell didn't you bring some amphibian tanks? You've got to get the tanks ashore quickly, and stay on schedule.'

Duval silently cursed his superior.

'The tank carrier is manoeuvring close to a small pier; if all goes well, we'll start unloading in half an hour.'

'Oh, all right, get on with it.'

He turned his attention to the southern front.

'Colonel Jackson, what's your position?'

'We're running an hour behind time, sir. Visibility is down to about ten meters.'

'Get a fucking move on. At this rate, it will be midday before we take Galway.'

***

There was an eerie silence in Eyre Square where the visibility was down to three metres. A small number of guards patrolled the centre city area. Ulick had given strict instructions that no effort should be made to oppose the enemy landing. He and Frank spent the night in Paulo's, awaiting confirmation that the enemy had landed. Frank tried to persuade him to leave the country.

He replied shortly. 'I'm staying with my people.'

'You will be no use to us, if you're behind bars?'

He smiled, remembering the last time he was behind bars.

'I'll take my chances. Paulo, another round if you please?'

Paulo was visibly upset. 'I've just been talking to Sister Agatha in the clinic. All the hospitals are preparing for an influx of casualties.'

At four o'clock the phone rang. Paulo took the call.

'Ulick, that was our boys on Aran. There's some activity in the bay, but with the fog, they can't be sure it's the enemy.'

***

The big Count waited impatiently for confirmation that his troops had captured Galway. His assistant entered.

'Well?' he demanded.

'We have just received confirmation that our forces have landed on the shores of Galway Bay. They are having major problems with the weather.'

'Imbeciles,' he roared. 'Send in Williams.'

'Yes, sir.'

Moments later, Williams entered.

'Proceed with the remainder of the plan immediately.'

'I think, sire, we should await confirmation that we have captured Galway.'

'You're not paid to think man,' he roared. 'Carry out your orders at once.'

He withdrew.

***

Chris Vance joined the President in the Oval Office.

'Brussels has just announced that USE forces have landed near Galway. We have no reports of casualties.'

Elaine Byrne looked old and tired.

'Where are our submarines?'

'They're south west of Kerry; twelve hours away.'

'So, we've lost, Chris.'

He didn't disagree. 'It would now take a full scale war to recapture Galway.'

She suddenly felt old and tired.

'The very idea of going to war with Europe is enough to make me sick.'

'What do the joint Chiefs think?'

'They're all for war, but it will take us at least twelve months to mobilise fully.

Chris, I want you to go to Ankara. We have to have oil: do whatever kind of deal you have to.'

'Even if it means withdrawing support from Israel? That would be very damaging politically.'

'Chris,'she shook her head sadly, 'It's now a national problem. Our survival may depend on it. It's very simple. Israel has no oil: we have to have oil.'

He spoke very quietly. 'Elaine, you know this will ruin your chances of re-election.'

'I know, Chris, but right now that's the least of my worries. We'll have to move the Sixth fleet and blockade Aran and Achill. If we can't have oil: the Count won't either.' She paused. 'Do you agree with me?'

He nodded heavily. 'I do, Elaine, I have to say I didn't think you would have the guts to make such a difficult decision.'

She tried to smile. 'Neither did I.'

He rose. 'I'll leave for Ankara immediately.'

***

Becoming more and more impatient, General Conti paced back and forth behind the computer operators. Dan watched quietly.

'What the hell is keeping them, it's nearly six o'clock?'

The radio telephone rang. He grabbed it.

'What the hell is keeping you, Major?'

'The fog is getting worse, sir, we have to move very slowly.'

'Where are you now?'

'In a town called Barna, about six kilometres west of the city.'

'Enemy forces?'

'We're not encountering any opposition.'

'Good, report when you've joined up with Colonel Jackson.'

He put down the phone and rang the Colonel.

'Progress report, Colonel?'

'We're approaching a place called Oranmore, sir. No opposition so far.'

'Join forces with Major Duval at the square in the centre of the city.'

On the bridge, Admiral Sebastian was half way through his fourth cup of coffee. He was quite annoyed that Galway would surrender to General Conti; that should be his prerogative, but the ass of a General insisted.

Suddenly, the screen in front of him started to flash.

'What is it? 'He demanded.

Captain Herzog replied. 'Four enemy aircraft heading this way.'

'Damn, sound general Quarters.'

Alarms screamed throughout the fleet; the gunners manned their guns. The Admiral donned his hard hat.

'What altitude?' he demanded tersely.

'Fifteen thousand feet. Shall I give the order to open fire?'

'According to intelligence, Joyc hasn't got fighters. How far away are they?'

'Twenty five kilometers and closing.'

The admiral made up his mind. 'Don't fire unless attacked. Everyone stand by.'

The captain picked up the phone and spoke to the gunnery chief.

'Prepare missiles for launching.'

The Admiral walked out on to the open deck and stood at the rail, holding his breath. Every second seemed like an hour. The Captain joined him. Any second now they could be in the middle of a blazing battle. Perhaps, he should have launched the missiles. Then, he heard the sound of approaching aircraft. Thank goodness for the fog. The sound increased. Now they were right overhead. A deck officer joined them.

'They've passed over, sir. They're heading east.'

He breathed out again.

'Keep them under observation.'

'Shall I stand down action stations, sir?'

'No, they might be back.' He turned to the Captain. 'Let's see how the attack is going?'

In the operations room, General Conti picked up the phone.

'Yes, Colonel.'

'We've taken the city, sir, but there seems to be a problem.'

'No difficulty I can't handle. I'm coming ashore immediately.'

He slammed down the phone before the Colonel could continue and turned to the Admiral.

'Would you like to join me? I think you should be present when I accept the surrender of Galway.'

He was anxious to mollify the old sea dog.

'All right, are we taking the helicopter?'

'Yes, we have just about sufficient visibility.' He turned to the Captain. 'Has the TV crew gone ashore?'

'Yes, sir, with the first division.'

Ten minutes later, the Syrosky helicopter lifted off and swung away to the north. The General, in full military uniform, displaying all his shining medals looked quite pleased with himself. This would earn him his third star, and probably put him in pole position to succeed C-in-C Bendes when he retired.

Looking very vexed indeed, Dan was sitting quietly across from him.

Hovering high above the city, the fog lightened sufficiently to enable the pilot identify the square below. Descending slowly, they saw the lines of tanks on both sides of the square, with five thousand troops standing to attention. Clearly, all military activity had ceased. The pilot circled and landed in the middle of the park in the centre.

The General hopped out and headed towards a group of soldiers and civilians standing in front of an office block. The TV cameramen focused on him, as he marched briskly towards a tall, elderly, angry looking gentleman in a long black coat. A large, silent crowd of civilians stood behind this man. He didn't look like Joyc; the cowardly President must have escaped. He wouldn't get far.

Pictures had just started going out live, world-wide. The colonel approached him; the general waved him away; General Conti knew his moment of glory had arrived: he was live on TV and no one was going to get in his way.

He approached the tall gentleman while the Admiral rushed up to get in the picture.

'Sir,' he spoke in a loud, firm voice. 'I call on you to surrender the City of Galway and the country of Hibernia in the name of Count Otto Von Vernher, President of the United States of Europe.'

The tall man glowered at him; then screamed in a high pitched guttural voice.

'You call on me to surrender the city of Galway?'

'Yes, sir.'

'You fool; this is not the city of Galway: this is the city of Bergin in Norway. Get your soldiers and tanks out of my city: at once.'

The general was dumbstruck. This couldn't be. The colonel appeared at his elbow.

'He's right, sir. I checked with operations. There's been a horrible mistake. I tried to warn you.'

The admiral began to back away, while the Colonel made frantic signals to the cameramen to get off the air.

Dan was beside himself with joy. He danced around clapping his hands. I told you, I fix ya, ya big bullies.

***

There was uproar in Paulo's crowded pub. Ulick, Frank and Paulo danced around singing the Hibernian National Anthem "The West's

Awake." Unnoticed, Ozzy wandered into this great party with a big smile on his face. Ulick spotted him immediately; threw his arms around him and continued to dance.

'Where have you been all night, Ozzy?' as if he didn't know.

'Here and there,' not wishing to tell a lie.

'Paulo,' Ulick shouted, 'a pint for Ozzy.'

***

The Count was livid. 'Imbiciles, fools, traitors. I'll have them all shot.'

His assistant handed him the phone.

'Admiral Sebastian is on the line, sire.'

He picked up the receiver as though he was going to crush it into smithereens and roared. ' Imbecile, fool. Get out of Norway. Find Galway and take it this time or you'll be shot for treason.'

He slammed the phone down. The worthy Admiral's effort to pass the blame hadn't succeeded.

***

President Byrne couldn't believe it. She rang Chris Vance who was just boarding at Dulles.

'Chris, this is almost a miracle. Go ahead with your mission. I'm calling a meeting of the Joint Chiefs and I'll address the nation in the morning.'

'That's fantastic, Elaine. It gives us a welcome breathing space.'

'Do you think we could risk ordering the Sixth Fleet to sail to Galway?'

'I wouldn't just yet. Let me see if I can do a deal with the Turks.'

'Good luck, my friend. Keep in touch.'

***

It was after nine in the morning when the party finally broke up.

Ulick announced. 'I'm going home to bed.'

'So am I,' Frank was having difficulty keeping his balance.

Ozzy wasn't too bright either. 'Me too.'

He left them and headed out the road towards the Rath. The sun was trying to burn off the haze and let its countenance shine on the wilds of Connemara. Ozzy trudged along slowly. He would have to sneak into his little house without being seen and sleep it off. He didn't hear the approaching car until it was too late. It screamed up behind him, hitting him, throwing him up into the air. As it accelerated away, his body crashed on to the grassy mound beside the road and he knew no more.

***

Shortly afterwards, two helicopters landed near Ulick's house. Eight heavily armed commandos leapt out, and raced towards the house. They crashed through the back door, charged through the house until they found Ulick's bedroom. He was fast asleep, in a very pleasant dream in which he was chasing the big Count with a pitch fork.

One of them grabbed him while another produced a syringe. Ulick was still very groggy.

'Danda – boy,' he muttered, but Dan didn't come.

He felt a sharp pain when the syringe was rammed into his arm and knew no more. Without a word, they carried his inert body to the helicopter, which took off and headed east.

Ella, driving home from class, saw the helicopter, but didn't realise its significance until she saw the broken back door. She ran through the house; distraught, crying out for Ulick. After a while, she calmed down a bit and rang Paulo.

***

Meskedra was awakened in the middle of the night by massive explosions coming from somewhere nearby. Getting up, he put on his robe and went downstairs, where most of the brothers were huddled together, fearfully. He led them towards the back of the hotel and out into the gardens. Then he realised what it was, but couldn't share his knowledge with them. Massive bombs were falling on top of the mountain, with thunderous explosions. Flames were rising a hundred metres into the air. He smiled to himself. Someone obviously believed the story about the missile silo.

'Are we going to be bombed, Boss?' Lurglurg asked fearfully.

'No, there's nothing to worry about. Let's have a drink and go back to bed.'

Such was their confidence in him, they settled down immediately, but only the boss was allowed brandy. Lurglurg passed around two bottles of PD to the others.

As Meskedra made his way back upstairs it occurred to him that Paulette had not returned. He wasn't concerned about the money: he missed her and that surprised him, because his emotions were always kept on a very tight rein.

***

Ozzy came too in a hospital bed, although it took him sometime to realise this. He had a bandage on his head and felt sore all over. He remembered being thrown up in the air but that was all. A young doctor, in a white coat, approached and felt his pulse.

'You're a lucky man to be alive. Can you tell me what happened?'

'I must have been hit by a car.'

He picked up the chart. 'What's your name?'

'I don't know.'

'Where do you live?'

'I don't know.'

'You don't remember anything before the accident?'

'No, where am I?'

'You're in the clinic in Moycullen. You have concussion but that will pass in a few days. You've also appear to have lost your memory. I'll look in on you in the morning.'

After he departed Ozzy looked around him. He was in a two bed ward. The other patient, a bearded burly middle aged man had his leg in plaster but appeared to be otherwise in good shape.

'What happened to you?' he demanded.

'Hit by a car, I think. What happened to you?'

'Knocked down by a tractor. I'm Ned Rowley, from out Letter Mullen way. I'll have a haul of compensation to get for this leg.'

Ozzy tried to digest that, but couldn't. A pretty young nurse approached him.

'Wouldn't you like a nice cup of tea and some toast?'

'Would a pint be out of the question?' he didn't know where that came from.

She smiled. 'It would tonight.'

'I'll settle for the tea and toast then.'

After she left, he lay back in the bed. Then he noticed a little, old man with grey hair and a long grey beard, sitting on the end of the bed.

'Who are you?'

'Do you not know me, Dan?'

'Dan, who he?'

'That's you. I've come to bring you home.'

The patient beside him followed this apparently one sided conversation in disbelief. Jaysus, this fellow is gone in the head, or he's after big money.

'I'm not going home with you, little man.'

'Would it help, if I called you Ozzy?'

'Ozzy, Ozzy who?'

A nurse approached with a device in her hands. Kingpa disappeared. Ozzy shook his head. Was there a little old man there?

'I just want to take your blood pressure again. We got a funny reading the last time.' She wrapped the sleeve around his arm and proceeded to apply pressure.

He watched the mercury going up in the glass. Up and up it went and then suddenly exploded. The poor nurse was astounded.

'Oh, my goodness, that never happened before. I'll have to talk to the Consultant. Do you feel all right?'

'Apart from a sore head, I'm fine.'

'He might want you to have an angiogram?'

'What's that?'

'It's quite painless. He just runs a tiny probe from your side into your arteries and has a look at your heart.'

'I don't think I'd like that.'

She reassured him.

'You'll be fine. I'll ask matron to have a word with you when she comes on duty.'

He lay back, satisfied now he didn't like this place. He settled down a bit and tried to ignore the reverberations of the straf coming from his neighbor's bed.

In the morning, a rotund, jolly looking nun approached and let out a cry.

'Ozzy, what happened to you?'

'Who you?'

'Don't you know me? Sister Agatha. Wait there, I'll ring Paulo and get him to come in.'

Bemused, he lay back. Kingpa resumed his seat on the end of the bed.

'They are going to operate on you, Ozzy.'

'You keep coming and going, little man.'

The other patient was convinced now that Ozzy was off his rocker.

Kingpa disappeared. Ozzy blinked twice, without knowing it, and disappeared too. Ned yelled for the nurse.

'Sister, sister, get the head doctor. He's gone, he's fucking disappeared. I'll be claiming for loss of memory too.'

The nurse stared at Ozzy's empty bed, before running to Sister Agatha.

'Alert security, nurse, have them search the clinic.'

She smiled to herself as the nurse rushed away. Of all people, Ozzy, you should have been delighted to avail yourself of our hospitality.

***

Ozzy, fully recovered, met Frank in Paulo's. Frank had just made a TV appearance in which he castigated the Big Count for kidnapping Ulick, and demanded his immediate release. The Count, as might be expected, denied all knowledge. Ozzy was puzzled. If Ulick so much as mentioned his name he would know immediately where he was. This must have happened when he was unconscious in the clinic. He left Paulo's early, but didn't return to the Rath.

***

The USE fleet sailed west of the Outer Hebrides, heading out into the Atlantic. The mood in the operations room was grim; the Admiral fumed at their failure to find the real Galway. He demanded regular position checks, and then re checks as he became more and more paranoid. Captain Herzog didn't escape his wrath. Dan, with his hands behind his back, walked behind the operators looking up at them from time to time: he was vexed. They were still hell bent on attacking his friends. He scratched his head. How could he stop them this time?

***

The big Count was devouring his breakfast flakes still fuming at the incompetence of his subordinates. He looked up, and suddenly spotted a little man standing on the other end of the long table. Could this be an assassin?

'Where is President Joyc?' Dan demanded.

The Count roared. 'Guards, guards.'

Two heavily armed guards rushed in.

'Yes, sir.'

He pointed at Dan. 'Shoot him, shoot him.'

The officer in charge looked puzzled.

'I don't see anyone, sir.'

'Are you blind man?'

'No, sir.'

'Give me the gun.'

He handed over his machine gun.

The Count didn't hesitate. He opened fire. Dan stood there while the bullets whizzed through him destroying priceless paintings and porcelain statuettes. The collie dog streaked out from under the table and disappeared through the door. The Count's eyes bulged in disbelief when Dan walked towards him, and pointed his index finger at him. Surprisingly, he got nothing. Normally he could obtain any information he wanted from the mind of another. Could it be that the Count was mindless as well as mad?

Dan allowed the big Count to hear him.

'I fix you, ya big bully.' He disappeared.

The Count turned to the officer in charge.

'Did you hear that?'

'No, sire.'

He handed him back the gun. 'Get out,' he roared.

They withdrew hastily.

He sat down heavily. The little nagging voice in his head was laughing at him again. Was there a little man there, or was he becoming like Gunter?

***

Dan caught up with the collie dog down by the lake. The dog looked at him critically for a moment and then spoke in a deep voice.

'You the fellow the Count was trying to shoot? I wish he wouldn't do things like that; it upsets my sleep rhythm.'

'I am. 'Dan replied. 'Why do you stay in a place like this?'

He considered it. 'The food's not bad. Who you?'

He pointed his index finger on his chest. 'Me Dan from country far away. The bad Count has taken my friend and I don't know where he's keeping him.'

He thought about it. 'I hear everything that goes on around here. I could tell you stories that would make the hair stand on your head.' He looked at Dan's tightly cropped hair. 'Maybe not. Every Friday night the Count plays with three beautiful women down in the summerhouse.' He paused and continued somberly. 'No one gets me a little bitch to play with.'

'What's your name?'

'Bismarck. No name for a thorough bred dog like me. All the bitches laugh at it.'

Dan was hoping his new friend would be able to help him.

'What would you like to be called?'

'Prince would be nice.'

'Very well then, I'll call you Prince.'

'That sounds nice.' He paused for a moment. 'You're a nice little man; would you take me home with you?'

He hadn't expected this. 'Maybe later but now I need your help.'

'I've very lonely here since madam and the young one left. He walks the stupid Labradors, but ignores me. I'm a full bred collie; I've papers to prove it and I'm still treated like a dog. Even have to sneak into town to meet some of the young bitches, not that the talent around here is up to much. They think I'm a snob because I live in a palace. What a high class bitch wouldn't give for a night with me!'

'Do you like your master, Prince?'

'No, he's mad off his head. I want to come and live with you.'

'I need your help first. I have to find my friend.'

'I could write a book about this place; the plotting, intrigue and skulduggery.'

'Do you have any idea where they might be keeping Ulick Joyc prisoner?'

'No, but I'll listen more carefully when they're talking.' He paused. 'The Count has a place on the island of Mainau.' He pointed with his snout. 'It's just over there in the middle of the lake. Maybe your friend is there.'

'I have to go now, Prince, keep your ears open.'

'You will come back for me. I know everything that goes on around here.'

'I promise.'

***

Dan was impressed with the Von Vernher estate on Mainau. With its high walls, tall gates and heavily armed guards, it was a virtual fortress. He walked through the beautiful tropical gardens and entered the cut stone mansion near the waterfall. Stopping for a while, he listened to the guards chatting among themselves. Then he wandered through the big rooms furnished with antiques and long red drapes. The walls were covered with paintings of seascapes; his little feet sank into the deep Persian rugs.

One of the guards emerged from the kitchen carrying a tray laden with food and headed down some steps to the basement. Dan cantered along behind him. Once in the basement, the guard put the tray aside while he opened an old steel door with a big key. Dan followed him into a very large well furnished, basement with barred windows, a comfortable looking bed, tables, chairs, settees and a separate bathroom. There was no TV or radio. A big man was sitting at the table, apparently reading a book. Dan got quite a surprise: this man looked exactly like the big Count. He put aside the book when the tray was placed on a table beside him. The guard walked quickly towards the door.

'If there is anything else you require Gunter, just ring the bell.'

He rose, his eyes flashing, and roared at the man. 'When I get out of here, I'll have the lot of you executed. And that includes my brother.'

Dan smiled to himself. He's just like the big Count. The two of them should be here together.

But Ulick wasn't there.

***

In a secure hospital cell, in a prison just outside Paris, the patient began to come round. The doctor sitting beside him filled his syringe and before Ulick could get his brain in gear, injected him once again. He sighed as he went back to sleep. The doctor checked the saline drip, before resuming reading his book. His orders were to keep this man alive and in good shape.

***

Meskedra's heart missed a beat when he saw his beautiful Paulette enter reception, accompanied by her taxi driver carrying two suitcases. He leapt up immediately and put his arms around her. Lurglurg smiled his approval. She was breathless. 'I got the last flight into Galway.'

'It's so good to see you. I was beginning to despair.'

'You don't trust me, Andre, my love?'

'With my life.'

She handed him one of the suitcases. 'This will help save your order.'

He handed it to Lurglurg. 'I'll take it to the bank in the morning. Lurglurg, will you give Paulette your best room?'

'Certainly, Boss. You're very welcome back to Turla, Madam.'

She grinned at him. 'Lurglurg, I'm too young to be called madam. I could use a bath.' She paused. 'Is there really going to be an invasion?'

'It looks like it. The enemy fleet was spotted off the coast of Donegal two hours ago. I hope you will join me for dinner.'

'I look forward to it, Andre, my love.'

There was something about the way she said "Andre" that puzzled him.

***

Chris Vance rang the President from Ankara.

'Elaine, the Turkish Premier, Machmoud is playing hardball; he won't opt either way until after the invasion.'

'In the meantime we don't get any middle east oil?'

'That's correct.'

'Should I order the sixth fleet to sail for Galway?'

'If you do, Israel will come under immediate attack. In any case it's a bit academic; the fleet couldn't make Galway before the invasion.'

'The Joint Chiefs want to destroy the Aran and Achill refineries in one massive airborne attack. What do you think?'

'I don't agree. If there's time, and it's getting very short now, I believe you should fly in a marine task force to guard the refineries. The Count daren't risk destroying them.'

She sounded very depressed.

'There isn't time; USE forces will be in Galway by tomorrow.' She paused, obviously very upset. 'Chris, I'm afraid we're heading into a long and bloody conflict. Mexico and Venezuela have agreed to provide sufficient oil for the coming year. When Galway falls, I'll declare a state of emergency and order a full scale mobilisation of our armed forces.'

'Where are our two nuclear subs now?'

'They're in situ west of Aran; there's no way they can stop the USE fleet. Come home as soon as you can, Chris.'

***

Paulette looked very attractive when she arrived for dinner in a low cut black dress that accentuated her perfect figure. Meskedra sensed there was something different about her very seductive smile. The large dining room was nearly empty; the last remaining guests cleared out before the invasion. Lurglurg instructed Brother Mungo to put up a feast fit for a king. After downing half a bottle of PD - much to Lurglurg's disgust - he served lobster in a white wine sauce with a good

Italian white wine. They passed on the desert in favour of coffee, at which stage Lurglurg left them alone. He was sure they would have plenty to talk about - he was right.

She couldn't restrain herself any longer.

'Dear Andre, I got a terrible shock when I visited your little town in Burgundy.'

He smiled and waited.

'I discovered that you died - fifteen years ago.' She smiled wickedly and leaned towards him. 'Who are you?'

He grinned wickedly. 'Paulette, I don't think I know who I really am.'

She smiled just as wickedly. 'Try me.'

This wasn't easy for a man who never talked about himself but it was important that she should understand.

'Dear Paulette, I'm sorry if I deceived you; I've been deceiving people for most of my life. I have never admitted that before.'

She smiled, putting her hand on his. 'Why not start at the beginning?'

'I'll try. I'm not even sure of my nationality. My mother, Margaret Coates was half Irish, half English; my father, Pedro Martini was half Italian, half German. I was born near Zurich. We were part of the famous Aldo Circus - always on the move - and nationality was never an issue. I speak five languages and I've even learned a few words of the Gaelic since I came here.

Mother and father were trapeze artists, you know, high wire. They were such a happy couple although they would have preferred to have more children. This didn't bother me because all the circus children were brought up together. We were one big happy, noisy, competitive family. They didn't pamper me. I was required to attend school; we had our own excellent tutors who doubled as cashiers and managers. There was no way we could attend normal school. It was a wonderful, carefree time. Little did we know the extent of the financial struggle to keep the circus going. That would come later.

We travelled through every country in Europe, enjoying the sights when we weren't riding the ponies, feeding and bonding with our elephants - do you know elephants are very affectionate animals? -

playing with Ham, the strong man and the clowns. We gave the lions a wide berth.

Father really should have been an artist. He never missed an opportunity to visit the most famous art galleries and exhibitions, often taking me with him. He started to paint, just for his own pleasure; but never made any effort to sell his work. He just piled them up in our bungalow in the Algarve, where we spent the months of January and February every year. Such happy times; swimming; relaxing on the beach, and just being together.

Mother didn't want me to spend the rest of my life in the circus; she wanted me to go to university to become a lawyer or a doctor. I think this was because there was always the fear the circus would be forced to disband; a really serious worry because circus people know no other way of life.

I haven't mentioned my Uncle Antonio. We were always a foursome. A big man, much taller than father, he was quite handsome in a rugged fashion. He loved animals and people, and yet, very few knew him. He was the famous clown "Umberto" and still is. A very quiet and sincere man, I think he hid behind all that grease paint. His father, my grandfather, had been the horse trainer. He died shortly after the war.

Father and uncle both loved my mother but she chose to marry father. This never interfered with the close relationship between the brothers and I do believe that mother loved both of them. Antonio never married. To please mother, I studied Law in Cambridge and qualified as a Barrister but my heart wasn't in it. I worked for a short time with a London practice.

Then that awful day, when the train carrying the entire circus crashed near Munich. Dear mother, father and many of my friends died. I know they would have wanted to go together, and I believe they are happy wherever they are. I was devastated, couldn't think straight, and moped around for months.

Thankfully, Uncle Antonio survived. He took me in hand; in fact, he took over the father role of many bereft families. Putting his arms around us, he shielded us as best he could. I spent months visiting the injured in hospital; some of their injuries were horrific. But life had to go on. We lost most of our horses and ponies: the tigers and elephants survived. The circus was in desperate need of funds.

I had learned to draw and paint from father, but wasn't in the same class. He once told me I could make a very skilful forger, such was my ability to copy anything I saw; but it was from Uncle Antonio I learned how to survive in this world. As a clown, he is a master in the art of disguise. He taught me well. As he often said to me. "If you dress like a lord and act like a lord, you'll be treated like a lord. If you dress like a tramp and act like a tramp, you'll be treated like a tramp."

He had an old friend, Julien Dupree, in the art world; as I was to find out, in the shady end of the business. He used to be a juggler in the circus until he rose to greater things. A rotund, elderly man he re-eked of garlic, although he dressed well. We took him to the Algarve to view my father's paintings. He was very impressed.

'As they stand, maybe ten to twenty thousand.'

'Euro?'

Julien nodded. 'The style is perfect. If the name "Rembrandt" appeared on each one - plus a little bit of ageing - it would be different. It could then be ten to twenty million dollars.'

'Are you serious?'

'Yes, that's the art world for you.'

'We'd never get away with it.'

He smiled. 'It happens every day. A hitherto unknown Rembrandt, Titian or Constable turns up. They are snapped up by greedy wealthy collectors who won't even show them to their friends.'

'How do we go about this?' Uncle Antonio asked.

'You need a good front man,' he surveyed me, 'Someone like this young fellow, handsome, honest looking and charming.'

I was shocked at first, but the circus was in such dire straits that we had to do something. The Bank wouldn't even talk to the Aldo family.

'What happens if the collector finds out?' Uncle asked.

'That's the best part. They usually don't want anyone to know they've been conned, so they don't call in the cops.'

Uncle used his life savings to finance the venture. The paintings were sent - by courier - to a highly reputable New York dealer who invited a small number of his special clients to view them. It was all very hush hush.

The most expensive suite in the Astoria was booked in the name of John Getty. Carefully disguised I flew, first class, to New York. Checking in at the hotel, the duty manager inquired politely "Any relation to J.P. sir? " I nodded knowingly and said, 'We'll keep quiet about that.' and handed him a hundred dollar bill. From there on I got the full VIP treatment.

It was nerve wracking but it worked. I stood around trying to look knowledgeable while experts examined the canvas for ageing and checked, or pretended to check, the subtlety of the brush strokes. I was lucky; one well known billionaire collector took all five pictures. A dollar draft was quickly transferred to a newly arranged account in Hamilton, Bermuda and I was on the first flight out of Kennedy. The twelve million dollars paid off the massive medical bills and saved the circus.'

Paulette poured more coffee.

'This is fascinating. Do go on.'

'I found the whole experience so exciting I couldn't stop. Uncle objected. He was afraid I would end up in jail. But he did insist on greater precautions, and for those, I would later be grateful.

I built up an array of identities with false passports and professional disguises. In the years that followed, I relieved greedy wealthy, sometimes billionaires, of large sums of money. Most of the money was invested in Wall Street for the circus and guarantees its sound financial continuity. I put some aside for myself because I knew I could not fulfil my dearest wish: I could not go back to the circus. Uncle employed an international firm of accountants to fend off awkward questions about the refinancing. I never took any money from the poor, but then the poor don't have any money.

After we met in Paris, I went to Rio, where I relieved a bank of several million dollars. Never did like banks. They didn't like me either and I soon discovered that the CIA and Interpol were taking a special interest in my activities. They didn't know what I really looked like; they never got my fingerprints, and I made a practice of never using the same identity twice. It was time for a career break, perhaps a permanent one.'

'How did you happen to come here to Turla?'

He smiled. 'In Rio, I met an elderly disgruntled Irishman who worked in the laundry here. I took him out for a few drinks; he told me he used to be a brother here; I think he was lonely, he talked for hours about the brothers; so much so, I felt I knew most of them when I arrived in Turla. I really don't know how he ended up in Rio; I think he had a drink problem. Anyway, he told me all there was to know about the order and its lack of contact with the Father house. I learned afterwards the Father house was destroyed during the first World war and was never reconstituted.

I still had to get out of Rio. Changing identity again, I left the luxury hotel and took up residence in a shack near the beach. I became a decrepit old tramp, and shortly afterwards moved into shantytown where I became a temporary resident. After careful planning, Brother Meskedra emerged, took passage on a tramp steamer to Cuba and eventually found my way to Ireland. The rest you know.'

She smiled and shook her head. 'What is your real name?'

'Take your pick.'

'You must know who you are?'

He grinned. 'Now, I'm Meskedra.'

'I know that but what was your baptismal name?'

'Do you know, I don't remember being baptised?'

'I can't keep calling you '"Andre."'

He grinned. 'How disappointing, it's plain Giovanni Martini.'

'I like it. Andre was a bit too pompous. Tell me what happened in Paris?'

'Fortunately, I followed my usual routine. I arrived as Baron Andre La Dorke, as you know. Then, I left the hotel very quietly and, an hour later, returned as the humble shy and retiring, Reverend Pierre Renaud from a little village near Boule and took a room under that name. I didn't attract any attention. I went to Andre's room, unnoticed, of course and took all but essential clothes to the Reverend's room. It sounds more cumbersome than it was; I always travelled light anyway. I had already made contact with my clients, three gentlemen who were going to buy the Eiffel Tower for scrap - from the Ministry.'

She laughed out loud. 'It was you?'

'Yes, posing as the special secret representative of the Minister, I was entrusted with this task. Plans were being drawn up, or so I said, in strictest secrecy, of course, to replace the tower with an even higher and more elaborate one. Why the secrecy? The Minister could not unveil his plans until after the forthcoming election as it would be a contentious project.'

'And you nearly got caught.'

He mused. 'Well yes, and no. I succeeded with the first two punters: not many people know that. Unfortunately, the third one had less pride than money and called in the police. You see now, why I had to get out fast. I got a call from the desk to say two gentlemen were on their way up. There followed a rapid exit; it was the first time I had to use this method of escape. I moved to the Reverend's room, where I became, once again the Reverend Pierre Renaud. It was quite funny. I was checking out while the police were interviewing the reception staff. They didn't even look at me.'

'And there was I, a humble con artist falling for another Houdini.'

'You were cute enough too, leaving a false forwarding address. I went to Milan looking for you but no one knew a Paulette Rossini in Milan.'

She grinned. 'You weren't the only one covering your tracks. You might have found me in Rimini if you were looking for plain Paula Sarti.'

'Paula, I like it: it's more aristocratic than Paulette. Tell me about yourself?'

'I was brought up by my beautiful actress mother. I never knew my father, but suspect the worst. Mother didn't tell me much about him, except that he came from a wealthy background; he was a playboy who never grew up. I wanted to be an actress too but I just hadn't mother's talent. So, I became an artist's model. That's where I met Francesco; I worked for him. He could copy any of the great masters, and dearly wanted to make some money for his approaching old age. A recognised expert in antiques, he taught me everything he knew. He was like a father to me. He lived alone in his attic studio after his wife died. He was a dear man - I felt so sorry for him. I had a fondness for expensive clothes; I still have, so it was easy to persuade me to operate as the front man. Francesco used to say they would be so busy admiring me they wouldn't bother to look at the paintings. We were very successful. Then, five years later, he died suddenly. I really miss him.

So, I became an antiques dealer and made a very good living out of it. Occasionally, I would be approached to make a discreet purchase; that's how I came to Turla, and look who's here before me. It must be fate. Mother married a wealthy film director and is now living in LA. I visit whenever I can.'

He shook his head smiling. 'So now I call you Paula?'

'It's very pedestrian after some of the exotic names I've used.'

'I like it.'

'Do you ever see your uncle now?'

'We meet once a year at an apartment I own in London. He's nearly seventy now. I've been trying to persuade him to retire to St Lucia where I have a villa but he isn't ready just yet.'

'And you've been here over six years.'

'I didn't intend to stay that long, but I got involved with the problems here and waited to help. It's funny, you know, they're such a wonderful collection of genuine, sincere and dedicated men; like some of the characters I knew growing up in the circus.'

'What's next?'

'My cover here has been blown although I think I can trust Nick Forde. I can't do anything until the invasion is over. Then, I suppose, I'll have to move on.'

She looked pensive for a moment.

'Nick Forde; I've heard that name. He's the fellow flogging copies of your missile plans all over Europe at ten million a time.'

He grinned happily. 'I hope no one tries to launch one of those missiles.'

She put her hand on his. 'Do you mind if I stay?'

'I would love that. I was afraid you would not like to be associated with such a scoundrel.'

She smiled. 'Didn't you say that only the great sinners go to Heaven?'

'I certainly qualify under that heading.'

'I'll deliver the plans and come back immediately.'

'I'll be counting the days, dear Paula.'

Dan, who had listened to the entire story, wondered if this was just another yarn. I do not trust you, Abbot Meskedra. Where is this place "Heaven" they talk about? I'll have to ask Kingpa.

***

Ulick was slowly coming to. Up there somewhere was the surface if he could only reach it. He didn't feel the jab of the needle. He knew no more.

***

Admiral Sebastian was becoming more and more paranoid; he confronted Captain Herzog in the operations room.

'Are you sure we're a hundred kilometres west of Aran?'

'Yes, sir. We've checked it thoroughly. Before dark, we had visual on the mountains of Connemara.'

'Have you any reports from Galway?'

'All quiet there, but intelligence tells us there are two American Submarines between us and Aran.'

'Does the Count know that?'

'Yes, sir. He says sink them and be in Galway by tomorrow evening latest.'

'So, we're going to war with America. I don't like this.'

'Neither do I sir, but orders are orders.'

'We have to be extremely careful not to damage the refineries.'

The Admiral looked at his watch. 'It's twenty two hundred now. I'm going to turn in for a few hours.'

***

The "Arizona" and "California" sat on the surface under a full moon; in the distance they could make out the lights of the fleet. Behind them, the oil refinery on Inish Mor stood out against the eastern sky: close by, like enormous beacons, three gigantic platforms bobbed up and down quietly in the calm sea. Five fully laden tankers sailed south under full steam, anxious to get clear of the area before hostilities commenced.

Captain Milken, a tough scrawny little man stood on the bridge and studied the fleet through his infra red binoculars.

'They will attack at dawn, Sam,' he spoke to his first officer.

'The Sixth had better get here and fast, sir.'

He hesitated. 'They're not coming, at least not yet.'

Sam was dismayed. 'We're taking on this bloody shower by our-selves?'

'The President's orders are to hold Aran.'

'Does she know what she's asking?'

'I think she does. Her son is a lieutenant on the Arizona. We had better go below and study the charts before I talk to Captain Ryder and see if we can come up with some kind of strategy that will give us a fighting chance.'

***

Frank and Ozzy met for a pint in Paulo's after the TV news an-nounced that the USE fleet was sighted off Aran.

Frank was livid. 'I phoned the British Prime Minister, Alan Ho-lland. He's been trying to contact the big Count to insist on a meeting of heads of States. The bloody bastard won't even take his calls.'

'So we're on our own,' Ozzy looked distinctly unhappy.

'I'm afraid so.'

'What are we going to do?'

'I'm going out to Aran with Paulo. I want to make sure none of our people get out of hand. Would you like to come?'

'No, I'll have another pint and go home.'

***

Admiral Sebastian didn't sleep very well. He dreamt repeatedly of a big man in a black coat shouting "This isn't Galway, you fool." He was awake when his personal assistant arrived with his coffee and toast.

'What does it look like out there, Seve?'

'Fog, senior, all fog.'

'Not again, but that won't stop me; nothing will get in my way today.'

Seve nodded and departed quietly.

At four thirty he joined Captain Herzog and General Conti in the operations room.

'Well gentlemen, this is the day. What about those two American subs?'

The Captain replied. 'Radar hasn't located them yet.'

'Does that mean they've gone?'

'No, sir, they could be silent on the rock shelf, or staying close to the oil rigs.'

He nodded. 'Are we all set to go forward at five?'

'Yes, sir. I've plotted a course that will take us in south of the Aran Islands.'

Together, they studied the charts while the seven operators watched their screens for enemy activity.

Satisfied, the admiral nodded to himself.

'Send the order to the rest of the fleet with course details.' He looked at his watch. 'Sail in ten minutes.'

The gigantic engines of the USE vibrated throughout the ship, followed by the siren for general quarters.

***

Just as the admiral was about to leave for the bridge one of the operators suddenly cried out.

'Sir, we have an enemy fleet, sitting just west of Aran.'

'Are you sure?'

'Yes, sir.'

'Let me have a look.'

He peered at the screen. Sure enough, a large number of pulses confirmed the presence of a massive fleet.

'Where the hell did they come from?'

'I don't know sir they weren't there a minute ago.'

'How many ships?'

'I make it twenty, but I can't say if they have any aircraft carriers.'

The Admiral was beginning to get that sinking feeling again.

'It has to be the American Sixth. Check with intelligence.'

'It can't be. Last we heard it hadn't left the eastern Med.'

He could feel the ship moving under his feet. 'Go to Action Stations immediately.' He turned to the operator. 'How far away is this fleet?'

'Twenty kilometers and closing. They're in range, sir.'

'Send a signal to all captains. 'Open fire in five minutes, and increase speed to all ahead full.'

The captain objected. 'Should we not proceed more cautiously, sir? We have no intelligence to go on.'

The admiral didn't like to be questioned.

'Captain, with our 133MM guns we have the most powerful fleet in the world. We'll go through this lot in no time.'

The Captain shrugged and walked away.

***

The sonar operator on the California alerted Commander Milken.

'Commander, we've got another fleet up top.'

'Our Sixth?'

'No, sir can't be. Has Hibernia got a navy?'

'Not that I know of. Send a message to Commander Johns. We will sit tight here on the bottom and let them fight it out.'

The operator grinned. 'I Never thought I'd be so happy to see the navy.'

***

The foggy morning's peace was suddenly disturbed by massive explosions when the USE fleet opened fire on the fleet guarding Aran. Salvo after salvo was fired as the gunnery crews used their computers to calculate target distances. For half an hour the firing continued without reply. Well satisfied, Admiral Sebastian walked out on to the open deck. It was going to be a major victory after all.

Dan, in his resplendent green admiral's uniform, with peaked cap - and an array of harp shaped shiny medals - paced back and forth behind him. The Captain joined the triumphant admiral.

'Admiral, we've scored massive direct hits on the enemy. Shall we continue firing?'

'Yes, continue the attack. I won't be satisfied until I've sent every one of Joyc's ships to the bottom of the ocean.'

The Captain left him.

Dan shook his little fist up at the great man.

Ya big bully. I show you. Finn, strike the flag and open fire.

The air was immediately filled with earth shattering explosions; shells began exploding all around the USE fleet, curiously, scoring no direct hits. Dan smiled when the Admiral ran for cover. Wave after wave followed, some crashing into the sea in front of the fleet, others in between the warships sending large spouts of water cascading high in the sky. The noise was deafening. Dan danced around clapping his hands with glee.

***

High above the Atlantic waves, in the old Dun Aengus fort on the western edge of Inish Mor; Frank, accompanied by Paulo, had listened, in dismay to the one sided naval battle: their eyes opened wide when they heard the massive response. A reporter and cameraman raced over to them.

'What the hell is going on, sir?'

It was Paulo who replied. 'You can tell your viewers that the Hibernian fleet has now gone into action defending our people.'

'We have a fleet?'

'Of course we have a fleet.' Paulo replied.

The reporter groaned. 'If only this damned fog would lift. I'm going to hire a boat and go out there.'

Over the deafening noise, Frank grunted. 'Don't get in the way.'

***

As the day progressed, the sounds of naval gunfire could be heard clearly in Galway; both sides increased their fire power. The admiral was becoming more and more unhappy. A phone call from the big Count hadn't helped.

"Charge them," he roared, "Wipe them out. Send them to the bottom of the ocean."

Dan hearing these dire threats, smiled broadly.

***

In the study of Von Vernher Castle, the big Count addressed C-in-C Bendes.

'General, launch the missiles and destroy that damned fleet.'

Bendes was a bit doubtful.

'Sire, you saw what happened the last time we launched missiles against these people. I think we should await the outcome of the naval battle.'

The Count roared. 'You're not paid to think. Launch the missiles.'

He persisted, handing him three large photos.

'Count, these are the photos taken after the bombing raid on the mountain covering Joyc's missile silo. As you can see, the mountain is completely undamaged.'

He looked at the photos, and threw them aside.

'Launch the missiles, dam you.' he roared.

The General left without even saluting.

Alone the great man ground his teeth. I am surrounded by fools, imbeciles and traitors. I'll double the guards again.

When he looked up, Dan was standing on a chair, the other side of the desk.

'Where is Ulick Joyc?' he demanded.

'Go to hell,' he roared, 'you exist only in my mind.'

Dan disappeared and reappeared sitting on the cabinet behind the Count.

'You very bad man, Count Otto, you do bad things. I fix ya.'

He let out a mighty roar. 'Guards, guards.'

They rushed in, guns at the ready.

'Yes, sire.'

He leapt up and looked behind him. Dan was gone.

'What are you doing here?' he roared.

'You called, sire.'

'I didn't call, get out,' he roared.

They left exchanging telling glances.

The big Count pondered. That voice again! Could it be?

***

Exhausted after his trip to the Middle East, Chris Vance reported immediately to President Byrne in the Oval Office.

'Is it true, Elaine?'

She looked a bit more relaxed. 'It seems that President Joyc has a fleet after all.'

'Can it hold the USE?'

'I hope and pray they can hold out until we fly in fifteen thousand Marines to Galway.'

'How soon will they be ready?'

'Three days.'

***

Dan found Prince down by the lake, in typical downbeat humour.

'I was afraid you weren't coming back.'

'Dan always keeps his promises.'

'Are you taking me away now?'

'Not yet. Have you found out where they're keeping Ulick?'

'His name was not mentioned, but I found out a whole lot of other things you might like to know. This is a very scary place.'

***

At three in the afternoon, with no sign of the fog lifting, Captain Herzog reported to the Admiral.

'Our logistics people say we should have disposed of the enemy fleet by now but if anything their fire power is increasing. If we maintain our current fire power, we'll be out of ammunition by noon tomorrow.'

'Right, let's get it done. Send our five battleships forward at full speed to engage the enemy at close quarters.'

'Yes, sir,' he departed.

The fog lifted a little; the five battleships moved forward. Dan frowned. What do I do now? I can't use force. He joined the gun crews as the battleships disappeared from view. Massive covering fire was continuing. He smiled to himself. When the next salvo was fired by his fleet, he pointed at one of the shells; it veered off course and crashed into the giant rudder of the leading ship. In quick succession, the four other attacking ships suffered similar damage. Unable to steer - dead in the water - they were forced to close down their engines.

Dan was quite pleased. I didn't do that, did I?

'Damage report?' the admiral demanded tersely.

The Captain returned a few minutes later.

'They're rudderless, all five, sitting ducks too badly damaged to do running repairs. We'll have to take them in tow.'

'Do it,' he ordered tersely.

'Shall we continue firing?'

'No. Contact supplies, order more shells, and find out what the hell is keeping our aircraft carriers?'

Five minutes later, the USE fleet guns fell silent. Dan's canon increased their firepower. Fifteen minutes later, he ordered his guns to stop firing.

He was beginning to fancy himself as an admiral.

As evening approached the fog lifted; the enormous crowd gathered on Dun Aengus, roared on the mighty Hibernian fleet carrying the Green flag; standing proudly and firmly between them and the enemy.

***

At the missile silo Rolf listened to the Commander's order in silence.

'You saw what happened the last time.'

'I did, but what can I do except carry out orders?'

'Haven't you got any influence over this madman?'

'No.'

'Well, I'm not carrying out any such orders. We're not at war with Hibernia.'

'Then I have to relieve you of your command, and put your assistant in charge.'

'That's fine with me. I won't be facing a war crimes tribunal when the people of Europe come to their senses and get rid of this lunatic.'

He cleared his desk and left the complex.

***

In the oval office President Byrne and Chris Vance were becoming more and more puzzled; she turned off the TV.

'We have no reports of a local fleet. What kind of fools are running our intelligence services?'

He wasn't so sure. 'Do you remember the famous Galway airport some years ago?'

'The one that had to be abandoned because of local opposition?'

'Yes. Joyc was involved in that campaign and many believe he was helped by the Little People who are said to live in a local Rath.'

'You surely don't expect me to believe in Leprechauns?'

'Some very strange things are happening. How could a modern fleet find itself in Bergen when it should be in Galway? A Hibernian fleet suddenly appears out of the mist. Commander Milken of the Arizona assured me it came from nowhere. Incidentally, they have moved out of the area, and are currently lying off Clare Island.'

'That's a relief. If the Count can't take Galway, maybe we can force him to the table. Some of the other member heads of states are thoroughly fed up, and would welcome any opportunity to ditch him.'

'That won't be easy.'

***

Admiral Sebastian sat in his armchair on the bridge and, using his powerful field glasses, looked angrily at the enemy fleet - comprised of twenty battleships, each armed with ten sixteen inch guns, and twenty five thirty inch guns - now in clear view, less than ten kilometres away, with the oil rigs and the cliffs of Aran in the background. When he looked again, his heart sank; the Hibernian fleet now had two aircraft carriers with fighter jets lined up for take-off.

He blamed Captain Herzog for their failures to date. Someone would have to carry the can; someone other than himself. When his mission was completed, he would demote the arrogant German American who tried to tell him his business.

The Captain, for his part, made no further effort to save the Admiral from himself. He could see an early retirement coming up for the text book Admiral. The first officer entered and handed him a message that he passed to the Admiral.

'Good, the missiles have been launched. It will give me great pleasure to see that damned fleet wiped out.'

Dan, who had been there for some time, waved his little fist at him. You big wind, I fix ya.

The admiral looked at his watch. 'They should be here in ten minutes. I want to watch the fireworks from the open deck.'

Getting out of his big chair, he sauntered out on deck, followed by the Captain and Dan. The chief computer operator raced out after them.

'Sir, the missiles, the missiles!'

'What is it man?'

'They, they're coming directly for us. I've alerted Munich. They can't control them.'

'You mean?'

'Yes, sir, we're minutes away from being wiped out.'

Red faced the Admiral screamed at the Captain. 'Do something - we've got to get out of here.'

The Captain would have enjoyed this were his own neck not also on the chopper.

'Too late, sir.'

'What can we do?' he screamed.

'Prayer might help, sir.'

Dan smiled as hundreds of missiles zoomed in out of the eastern sky.

Throwing himself on the deck, the Admiral started to blubber aloud.

'Mama Mia, Mama Mia, save me.' the Admiral moaned. 'Jesus help us.'

The Captain stood his ground: he would die like a man.

Dan was of two minds; then, he pointed his finger at the approaching missiles. At the last second, they changed course and plunged into the sea in a series of massive explosions, sending millions of tons of water cascading over the fleet.

Dan danced around clapping his hands. Three sailors lifted the blubbering Admiral off the deck and carried him to the bridge. I told ya, I'd fix ya, ya big bully.

***

With the stand-off in the Atlantic, if one may use such an expression about a naval impasse, life in Galway returned to normal, at least for the present. Meskedra and Lurglurg presented themselves at the resumed hearing in the Galway Circuit Court unaware that Dan the doubtful was also present. He could not be convinced that Abbot Meskedra was on the level, a new expression he picked up from Ulick, but he liked Paula; she was a genuine rogue.

With a benign expression, Big Bishop Brennan sat quietly at the back of the court, clearly satisfied that this time he would have no difficulty getting his way. He would have the brothers out of Turla on the next coach. It would be a most prestigious residence for a prince of the church.

Judge Ivers listened to the long rambling opening speech delivered by BBB's counsel that ended when he put the all important letter into evidence by handing it to the Clerk, who placed it before the judge. He examined it briefly and put it down in front of him.

Silke concluded. 'Accordingly, Your Honour, I submit that from the evidence before you, my client is entitled to an order for possession of the Turla estates.'

'Mr Silke, do you intend to call your client?' The judge inquired.

'No, Your Honor, it wouldn't be fitting to ask my lord Bishop to take the stand.'

The judge's voice was tinged with sarcasm.

'And why not, Mr Silke? Some corroborative evidence would be helpful.'

BBB rose impatiently. 'I'll take the stand. Let us get this matter finished without any further nonsense.'

Duly sworn in, he took the stand.

His counsel rose. 'Your Honour, I have no questions for my lord Bishop.'

The judge looked at defence counsel.

'Mr Walsh.'

Meskedra's counsel rose. He didn't like the way this was developing.

'My Lord Bishop, how did this document come into your possession?'

'It came to me from my predecessor and to him from Bishop Jarlath.'

'Is there any way you can verify the signature, or tell the Court why the Abbot of an order that bought and paid for Turla should sign such a document?'

He responded impatiently.

'That's irrelevant. You've seen the document: that's the end of the matter.'

'I see, my Lord Bishop, and why do you want this estate?'

'That, sir, is none of your business. But I don't mind telling you, I'm concerned about the immoral activities of these brothers.'

Judge Ivers mouth tightened. He was trapped, and he knew it.

'Thank you, my Lord Bishop.'

BBB sat down beside his solicitor.

The judge looked at Meskedra's counsel.

'Mr Walsh, I don't appear to have any option in this matter.'

Pat McDermott, the manager of the Lynch Bank, walked forward holding up a document.

'Your Honor, may I be heard?'

'Certainly, Mr McDermott, take the stand.'

Silke rose. 'I object, Your Honor.'

'Save your objection until Mr McDermott enlightens the Court.'

He nodded to Pat McDermott.

'Your Honor, I have here a High Court Order for possession of these premises and estates.'

Silke jumped up. 'Your Bank has been paid in full, sir. You have no interest here.'

The witness smiled thinly. 'No, sir, my bank has not been paid. I still have a mortgage on Turla for more than five million.'

BBB looked extremely angry.

'Your Honor,' Silke retorted, 'I have been misinformed. I believe a further adjournment will be necessary to enable my client consider his position.'

Dan started jumping up and down, not that anyone was aware of his presence. Adjourn, adjourn, this will go on forever.

He pointed at the document sitting on the Judge's bench. A sudden draught of wind blew it up into the air. BBB tried to grab it and, in doing so, fell on top of the Court clerk. Up and up it went towards a window high up in the chamber and disappeared out the window. A mad scramble followed, led by BBB who pushed people out of his way in a most un-dignified manner. He led the cavalcade from the chamber. Out the front door they raced, around the side of the old nineteenth century building.

By now, the letter was flying towards the salmon Weir Bridge nearby. Traffic thundered by in both directions. BBB didn't hesitate. He raced across the road, waving his humble followers to stop. Dan cantered after them, smiling broadly. As they reached the bridge, the document flew gracefully down into the rapids below and disappeared.

When everyone recovered, the Court resumed.

Silke rose. 'Your Honor, the lack of the letter doesn't change anything.'

Judge Ivers. 'You're right, Mr Silke it doesn't change anything: it changes everything. I have no option but to rule in favor of the Brothers, and consider Mr McDermott's High Court Order.'

'Leave to appeal, Your Honor?'

'Denied.' He turned to Pat McDermott. 'Well, Mr McDermott let me see your order.'

He allowed himself a little smile. 'Your Honor, I no longer need to serve this Order.'

'Why?'

'I have just been handed a draft for the full amount of our mortgage.'

'May I ask by whom?'

'The Abbot Meskedra.'

The judge permitted himself a little smile. 'That's the end of the matter then. This court is adjourned.'

BBB stormed out of the chamber.

Dan, with puzzled expression, scratched his head. I couldn't be wrong about Meskedra could I?

***

The Big Count was furious. 'Imbeciles, fools, traitors,' he bellowed thumping the desk in his study. 'I'll have them all shot.'

C-in-C Bendes flinched, reluctant to convey the rest of his news.

'Sire, the Americans and the British want a peace conference.'

'A peace conference, are they mad? Order that fool Sebastian to destroy the enemy fleet and take the oil refineries immediately.'

'Sire,' he spoke quietly, 'Admiral Sebastian is almost out of ammunition, and five of his warships are disabled.'

He roared. 'Then get rid of him, and get me a real admiral.'

'Sire, we're going to have to reinforce the fleet, and send two aircraft carriers.'

'Do it.'

'Sire, it will take weeks.' He paused. 'If you agree to a peace conference it will give us time to prepare for a massive invasion.'

A crafty glint appeared in the great man's eyes.

'Oh, all right, set it up.'

'There is one catch, sire. The Hibernian people won't agree unless we release Joyc.'

'Joyc, Joyc, who is he?'

'Their President.'

'Did we not execute him?'

'No, sire.'

'Then execute him immediately.'

'I don't think that would be wise, sire?'

'Damn you, you're not paid to think. Just carry out my orders.'

General Bendes departed.

Dan, who was present for the entire conversation, let the big Count see him.

He shook his tiny fist at him. 'You bad man, I fix ya.'

He disappeared before the Count could react. He still didn't know where they were keeping Ulick.

'You don't exist, except in my mind,' he muttered while he stared at where Dan stood a few seconds earlier.

***

Ulick was coming to very slowly again. 'Dan' he muttered. Putting aside his book, the doctor filled his syringe in preparation for another injection. Dan appeared beside him; snatched the syringe, and was almost overcome by a mighty urge to plunge it into the medic's ample arse. Instead, he kept moving the syringe around, keeping it just outside the doctor's reach. He tried to snatch it and, in doing so, unbalanced, tripped over the chair and started to fall on his rear end. Dan smiled holding the syringe upright on the floor. Sure enough, the doctor sat down on it with all his weight. He let out a ferocious scream and collapsed.

Dan grinned as he shook Ulick.

'Wake up, Ulick; I've come to take you home.'

He looked at him, still very groggy. 'What's happening, where am I, lad?'

There was a great commotion outside the cell.

'Talk later, take my hand.'

Ulick disappeared; Dan eased him through the wall into the adjoining cell as the door burst open and three policemen entered. Ulick was in bad shape, still in his pyjames with a long disheveled beard. Dan helped him into a bunk, and let him rest for a while. Alarms were now going off all over the prison.

Ulick listened quietly while Dan brought him up to speed.

He was astonished. 'I've been here for the past two weeks?'

'Yes, now we go home.'

'How are we going to get out of here?'

'We put blanket around you; no one see you.'

'Ready when you are, lad. I know you won't let me down.' He was thinking a bit straighter now. 'Where did you get a fleet?'

Dan smiled and pointed his index finger at his chest. 'My fleet. Admiral Dan, that me.'

'I shouldn't have asked.' He eased himself slowly on to his feet. 'Let's go.'

Leaning a hand on Dan's shoulder, they walked out of the prison together, past policemen running around like headless chickens, and took a train into the centre of Paris. Late in the evening, they found themselves walking down the Champs Elysee with window shoppers. Dan stopped when he saw a very well dressed model in a gent's outfitters.

'Come, we go in.'

They walked through the closed door, and found their way to a fitting room quite close to the window. Ulick sat down and rested. Dan opened the door into the window display, unaware that several window shoppers were admiring the goods on offer. He removed the coat, tie, shirt, vest, trunks and trousers from the model and brought them, one by one, to Ulick. They were a perfect fit. The window shoppers couldn't believe their eyes, as they watched the model, as it were, undress and the clothes leave the window of their own accord. One of the tourists was quick enough to get it on video. When removing the shoes and socks, Dan noticed the astonished shoppers staring at the bare full frontal model. Naughty people! He turned around the model so that he now had his arse to the gapers.

Before they left, Ulick wrote a note instructing the shop to send the bill to him in Galway. Smiling, they walked out past the gapers who insisted loudly they saw the model do a strip.

They strolled across the Champs Elysee until they came to a luxury hotel.

'We go in,' Dan said.

'I've no money.'

He took him by the hand. 'We not need money.'

Dan led him to, what he called the 'moving floor' and they went up to the tenth floor. Leaving Ulick, he walked through the rooms until he found an empty one. Now, they could relax.

'I need a shower, a shave and a pint,' Ulick was getting more with it.

He picked up the phone, rang room service and ordered steak, onions and spuds for both of them with lashings of coffee. While they waited, he showered and, finding the necessary equipment, shaved.

'I must ring Ella; she'll be worrying about me.'

He rang his home. Ella was so happy to hear from him. He assured her he was in no danger and promised to come home as soon as possible.

Afterwards, he switched on the TV.

'I feel a bit more human now.'

There was no mention of his escape.

'I had better ring Frank.'

While they were talking a waiter arrived, wheeled a large table into the room and served their meal. Dan looked out on the street below. A number of police cars were parked outside the outfitter's shop across the street. He smiled to himself; the big Count won't like this.

They tucked in to the tasty meal. Ulick left on the TV news.

Their attention was diverted by the announcement of a News Flash.

"We are going immediately to Galway where the Hibernian Deputy Premier, Frank Carney, is giving a news conference."

The picture showed a determined looking, Frank facing a small crowd in Paulo's.

'I have just received word that our President, Ulick Joyc, has escaped from a Paris prison where he was being detained - illegally - by Count Otto Von Vernher. We will now take part in the peace talks to be held in Paris in two days time. The Hibernian delegation will be led by our President, and we will be demanding the immediate resignation of Count Otto Von Vernher.'

A reporter raised his hand.

"Mr Carney, Count Otto's press secretary has denied they were holding Mr Joyc or that he escaped."

He responded sarcastically. 'How could they deny he escaped if they weren't holding him? I've talked to Ulick. I'll be meeting him in Paris tomorrow.'

***

The Count was so angry; it looked as if he was going to explode.

'Imbeciles, traitors: get him, turn Paris upside down if you have to,' he roared at C-in-C Bendes.

'Sire, if he makes it to their embassy, we won't be able to take him into custody.'

'Why not?' he screamed.

'Well, sire, apart from the fact that he has diplomatic immunity, we cannot enter the embassy without invitation.'

'Rules, rules! They don't apply to me,' he roared. 'Tell their damned Ambassador that I, Count Otto, order him to hand over Joyc to me at once.'

He knew this could not be done; he also knew the Count couldn't be told that.

'Yes, sire, I'll attend to it.'

'Is the new fleet ready yet?' he demanded.

'It won't be able to sail for another month.'

'Order them to be on their way to Aran by Tuesday.'

'Yes, sire.'

***

Meskedra was just finishing his packing when Paula arrived, looking absolutely stunning. It was time to move on. His emotions were very mixed, but the order was secure for the future and he would be in touch from time to time. He enjoyed his time in Turla; he had come to look on the brothers as his family; the previous night, he sat them down with them and explained that Lurglurg would be in charge for the future. They were quite happy with that arrangement and, now that the war looked like ending, the hotel business should pick up again. His final instruction to Lurglurg was to increase the price, or rather the offering required for the PD brand.

He and Paula would be starting a new life together and, perhaps, they would one day have their own family. Uncle would join them in their new home in St Lucia. Paula looked quite pleased as she admired his blue pinstriped suit, white shirt and red dickey bow.

'You look like a medical consultant, my love.'

'How did you guess? I'm now Dr Edwardo De Largo from Madrid, Spain and I have papers to prove it.'

'Did you tell the brothers about your past?'

He shook his head.

'Like true Christians they're only interested in the future.'

With a gleam in her eyes, she inquired wickedly. 'Have you any more copies of the missile plan?'

'Now, Paula, we're out of the game for good, and that's final. I'm going to sit on the beach and paint, something I always wanted to do.'

She smiled undaunted. 'That sounds wonderful. It's just that I happen to know a dealer in Cairo who would pay well for a copy of the plans.'

'No, no, my love we've retired, we don't need money. Let's say farewell to the brothers.' He paused and grinned. 'I might just have one copy left.'

At reception, they were greeted by the brothers, who tried to conceal their sorrow at seeing their much admired, if little understood Abbot, depart. He took Lurglurg aside and pressed two keys into his hand.

'Those are the keys of two safe deposit boxes in the Lynch Bank in Galway. If you ever have any financial problems there's enough there to see you right.'

He took the keys. 'You will come back to see us again, Boss?'

He nodded, to his surprise, close to tears. 'You're the Boss, now.'

Lurglurg did something he could never afterwards explain to himself or anyone else. He put his arms around him and hugged him. Then he hugged Paula.

'God keep you both.'

They were escorted to the waiting taxi. As it sped away, they stood waving sadly.

Dan who witnessed the farewell shook his head. Wily Meskedra, or whoever you are, you have restored my faith in mankind.

Lurglurg entered reception, followed by the others, and sat down on Meskedra's armchair.

'The traditions of our beloved Abbot Meskedra must be maintained.' He paused. 'I'll have a large Brandy and a Havana cigar.'

'Yes, Boss.'

'And move my things to the tower apartment.'

***

The big Count and his entourage flew to Orly in the USE Presidential jet. There, they were met by over a thousand security troops, two tanks, armoured cars and the Count's specially built, bullet proof Mercedes. A small crowd misread the massive show of force: mistaking paranoia for arrogance. The Count no longer trusted even those closest to him, not that he ever had. C-in-C General Bendes was in charge of the security arrangements. The cavalcade left immediately for the Luxembourg Palace.

Meanwhile, Frank's arrival at Charles De Gaulle Airport was greeted by thousands of Europeans, who admired the people of Hibernia for their courage and persistence in refusing to give in to the big Count. He declined to give a press conference but agreed to say a few words to the assembled media.

'Thank you, for your welcome. Now, that Ulick Joyc, our President has escaped, we will proceed quickly to remove all threats against our country. No, I'm not going into detail. What we have to say to the big Count, we will say to his face. Thank you.'

Whisked away quickly, they met Ulick and Ozzy in Sam Maguire's pub where a great party was in progress. Thousands of cheering Parisians filled the streets outside, watched by a large police force that knew better than to try to take Ulick into custody; not that they wanted to. They didn't like the big Count either.

Frank was furious when he surveyed Ulick's dishevelled figure.

'You must have lost a stone weight. We'll have to do something about that.'

He grinned happily. 'Nothing that a few pints won't cure.'

Frank was thinking ahead. 'How are we going to get you into the Luxembourg Palace? The big Count says you will not be allowed to attend.'

'We'll worry about that tomorrow. How are the people holding up at home? How is Ella?'

'She's fine; wanted to come, but I thought it best she stay at home.'

'You're right; this is no place for her. Moxy?'

'The cute hoor decided not to come. He thinks we'll make a balls of it and he'll be the beneficiary.'

'He could be right. I hear the entire conference will go out live on WTV?'

'The big Count insists. He plans to make us look like fools.'

Ozzy piped up. 'Ulick, do you think you should bring your own jug of water this time?'

After Ulick departed, Frank ordered more drinks. He was surprised when Bartley Higgins, Editor of Galway's national daily paper, "The Connaught Tribune" tapped him on the shoulder.

'How did you get over here, Bartley?'

'Walked all the way,' he paused and laughed. 'How do you think? I was on your flight. Is there any chance of getting me into the conference tomorrow?'

'I'll see what I can do.'

'What about Ulick's secret weapons? Has he really got them?'

'What do you think?'

He grinned. 'When our fleet turned up off Aran, I stopped thinking.'

'I can tell you certain things but not for publication.
'I'll settle for that. What is a Paddywhat-ever?'
Frank grinned.
'It's a machine for hurling bullshit at the moon.'

***

A great crowd gathered outside the Luxemburg Palace to watch the arrival of a long line of black Mercedes; one by one they dropped off their august passengers. New Panzer 65 Tanks were parked around the perimeter; heavily armed troops patrolled the grounds. Then, along came Sam Maguire in his old yellow Volkswagen rust bucket with Bartley and Frank who got a special cheer when he waved to the crowd. Armed guards checked to make sure Ulick was not in the delegation.

In the entrance hall, Frank was met by Chris Vance, Premier Holland of Britain and Premier Olaf Friedrickson of Norway. They greeted one another cordially. Led into the great hall, they found the Count sitting on one side of the long mahogany table - as on the previous occasion - flanked by the Heads of States still loyal to him.

The Commissioners and senior members of the bureaucracy sat quietly behind their leaders. Bartley and the other accredited journalists were accommodated in a cut off area at one end of the hall. C-in-C General Bendes sat nearby, satisfied with the security precautions he had put in place.

On Frank's side, there were four chairs. This time, jugs of water were provided. They marched forward boldly and stood facing the Count, who looked very composed in a dark blue suit. The cameras started to roll.

'Gentlemen,' the Count began affably, seeing Ulick wasn't present. 'You are welcome to this peace conference, which I have summoned in the interests of peace in our Community.'

'Hold it, right there,' Frank barked, 'we'll need another chair on this side.'

'Why?'

'President Joyc will be joining us presently.'

The Count smiled. 'Let me assure you that President Joyc will not be joining you, but you may have an extra chair.'

He paused while an extra chair was provided.

'Gentlemen, let us begin by examining the legal history of these United States of Europe to date, starting with the treaty of Rome and all subsequent Treaties and the powers they devolved on the executive.'

Frank leapt up angrily.

'We haven't come here to spend weeks raking through your small print. Get your fleet out of our national waters.'

The Count ignored him.

'We will continue.'

There was a loud gasp when Ulick suddenly appeared sitting beside Frank.

'Yes, Count, you would like to waste our time here while you prepare another fleet to attack our country.'

The Count almost choked. The rest of Frank's delegation rose and shook hands with Ulick while a happy looking Dan climbed up on the table and danced around clapping his hands.

'They still look like dummies.' he remarked to Ulick.

The Count leapt up. 'Arrest that man,' he roared.

Chris Vance rose as guards approached. 'If anyone lays a hand on President Joyc, this conference is at an end.'

That wouldn't suit him; he sat down, but continued to glower at Ulick.

Taking the Count's angry stare, Ulick looked at the team on the opposite side of the table.

'Don't blame the Count for your present predicament; blame yourselves for handing over control of your countries which wasn't yours to give, to this latter day Nero. We're a small nation on the edge of Europe; we value our freedom; we'll fight for it if we have to and we'll see off this power hungry jackal.'

Dan danced around clapping his tiny hands. The Count's face got redder and redder: his eyes bulged all the more.

Ulick raised his voice.

'Get out of our national waters before we send your fleet to the bottom of the Atlantic.'

The Count jumped up so fast his chair overturned behind him.

He bellowed. 'We'll settle this once and for all: name your weapon.'

The crowd gasped.

Premier Holland objected. 'Duelling has been illegal for the past two hundred years.'

He roared in reply. 'It's legal, if I say it's legal, and I say it's legal.'

There was a shocked pause. Everyone knew he was one of the finest marksmen in Europe. Dan scratched his head then walked down the table to Ulick and whispered in his ear. Ulick brightened up.

'Count, if I win this duel, will you accept that my country is an Independent State and withdraw your fleet from our shores?'

He sneered in reply. 'When this duel is over, you will be dead.'

'Answer my question.'

'Yes, Irish, I accept your terms. Name your weapon.'

'And you will resign as President of the USE?'

He nodded.

Frank snapped at him. 'Say it, damn you, so everyone can hear it.'

'Yes,' he thundered, 'but I won't lose.'

Chris Vance whispered to Frank. 'Is this wise?'

'I don't know.'

The Count goaded Ulick. 'What's keeping you? Name your weapon.'

Ulick spoke clearly and without hesitation.

'This conflict started over the humble pint of Guinness but it was always about much more than that. It was, and is about the right of free men and women everywhere to live their lives in peace. So, let this war end. I challenge you, Count Otto, to a pint drinking competition: the last man standing wins.'

The crowd gasped, many laughed, but the Count wasn't one of those.

He roared. 'That's not a weapon.'

Frank goaded him. 'You gave the man the option, are you afraid of him?'

'I fear neither god nor man. So be it.' He roared.

Frank continued.

'The competition will be held here at seven thirty tonight.'

Ulick winked at Dan. 'Let's get back to Sam Maguire's. I'm dying for a pint.'

***

Despite the fact that he was in much better shape than his opponent the Count decided to take no chances. He summoned his doctor and outlined his requirements; two hours later the doctor returned and handed over a small box of pills.

'Take two before you start sire, and two more after every four pints. They will do the trick but you will have a sore head tomorrow.'

'Tomorrow doesn't matter.' He lowered his voice. 'Is there any means of doctoring a barrel of Guinness without it being noticed?'

He smiled. 'It's a simple matter to inject through the cork seal.'

'Prepare the syringe, and return as soon as possible.'

'This will only work sire, if you're using separate barrels.'

'Do it.'

The big Count smiled to himself as the doctor departed.

Dan, sitting on the window, looking very vexed shook his tiny fist at him. You bad man, I fix ya.

***

A special counter and barrel rack were erected in the centre of the great hall; barrels of Guinness were rolled in and placed on the rack. A tradesman put taps in the barrels; glasses provided the workman departed.

Later, the doctor entered, looked around carefully to make sure he was alone. Then, extracting a syringe from his bag he injected its contents into one of the barrels. He left, as quietly as he came. Dan shook his head. There's no honesty.

***

The crowd outside the Luxembourg Palace cheered wildly when they saw Ulick sitting beside Frank in the back of Sam Maguire's car as it chugged slowly and noisily through the ornate gates. Frank was worried; Ulick was still weak after his ordeal. Ulick was worried for a different reason; he hadn't seen Dan. for the past three hours.

The great hall was crowded; TV coverage commenced when Ulick entered, escorted by Frank, Chris Vance, John Holland and

Premier Olaf Friedrickson. The Count's supporters looked worried; if he fell, they wouldn't last long and they knew it. Ulick took his place on one side of the counter; his adversary on the opposite side. A servant filled a pint of Guinness from each of the barrels; put one before the Count and the other before Ulick.

Frank objected immediately. 'Both pints have to come from the same barrel.'

Chris Vance understood. 'Take away both barrels, and bring just one.'

Ulick was relieved to see Dan had joined him, but the little man was jumping up and down beside him yelling, 'no, no.'

'What's wrong, lad?'

'I've already switched the barrels.'

Ulick got the message. He looked at the two pints on the counter.

'We can start with these two,' picking up both glasses he put his one before the Count and took the Count's one himself.

The Count's eyes opened wide. 'We wait for the new barrel.'

Ulick glared at him. 'I bet we do.'

***

When the new barrel was installed, they started all over again. Taking things gently, they got through the first four pints in less than an hour. Dan wandered around, looking suspiciously at those present. The Count was too confident. Had he set another trap?

The Count stopped. 'I need to visit the bathroom.'

Frank nodded agreement. 'Provided you're escorted by Premier Holland.'

He agreed and they left the hall together.

Arriving at the toilets, the Count entered one of the cubicles and locked the door firmly behind him. Once in, he extracted the small pill box from his pocket; somehow, it leaped out of his hand and disappeared. Dan smiled, and allowed the Count to hear him, 'Cheat, cheat, cheat.'

Leaving the toilet he muttered aloud, 'I am not a cheat.'

'You said something,' Holland asked.

'No, no.'

They resumed. By number ten, Ulick was beginning to sag a little; the Count noticed it.

'Come on, Irish, you're not able for me.'

Dan grabbed Ulick by the leg. 'Stay awake; don't let this big bully beat you.'

Ulick roused himself and glared at the Big Count.

'I'm only getting into my stride,' he retorted manfully.

That seemed to help him; they stayed head to head up to fifteen, when both were beginning to show the strain. Ulick paid a visit to the toilet and picked up a bit over the next few drinks. He had long since lost count of the numbers; not for the first time in his career.

Dan's acute senses were picking up all kinds of strange and conflicting vibrations. Something was wrong. The two contestants proceeded slowly. Then he spotted a tiny movement on the darkened balcony above. Going to investigate, he found a man with a rifle crouched down against the railings aiming at someone below. His head was about six inches from the railings; he didn't appear to be in any hurry to fire. Dan moved closer; his eyes opened wider; the gunman was aiming at the Count. How could that be? As the man prepared to fire, Dan knocked his head against the railings. The gun fired as the man collapsed. There was consternation below. Guards raced up and grabbed the culprit. The bullet had whizzed harmlessly over the heads of the crowd below. Dan rejoined Ulick while the unconscious gunman was removed.

The contest continued. At eighteen, both contestants were on automatic, scarcely aware of anything except the need to keep going. Then it happened: Ulick, still holding the counter with his right hand, sank slowly to his knees. The crowd gasped. Dan grabbed him, using all his strength. 'Come on Ulick, get up, get up; don't let this bad man beat you.'

The Count, swaying back and forth, in bad shape too, saw his opportunity. Raising his fist he banged it down on Ulick's fingers. There was a shocked hush. Somehow, the pain got through to Ulick. Very slowly, he pulled himself up and faced his adversary. Picking up his glass, he drained it slowly. It took the Count another minute to finish his drink.

'Two more,' Ulick demanded.

He tried to stare at the Count who seemed to be moving, or maybe he was seeing double.

'You're finished, Count.'

He took a slug of his drink. The Count did likewise. The end was very near now but there was no telling who would go first. Dan stood with his arms around Ulick's leg trying to give him some support. The atmosphere became tenser. Frank held his breath.

They took two more gulps; the Count put down his glass unsteadily, spilling some of its contents: he leaned against the counter. Ulick looked about finished. Then, very slowly, the Count went into free fall and ended up on the flat of his back on the floor. For all of five seconds there was absolute silence in that great hall. Then, a great cheer went up; Frank came forward.

'Well, that's the end of Count Otto.'

Ulick collapsed into his arms muttering, 'I will never give in to that big Count.'

C-in-C General Bendes stepped forward, drew his Magnum, and fired three rounds into the ceiling. Everyone dived for cover. The doors burst open; a hundred heavily armed soldiers rushed in and lined up along the wall.

The C-in-C made sure he was on camera.

'In the interests of the people of the United States of Europe, I am declaring a State of Emergency and devolving all power to myself as Supreme Commander of the Combined Armed Forces.'

There was a shocked hush. Frank turned on him.

'You can't do this.'

He glared at him. 'I've already done it. Stand back. You and many of your friends will be put on trial charged with high treason.'

The doors to the outer chamber were thrown open again, and a familiar looking man, accompanied by a regal lady - surrounded by armed guards - entered and marched forward. They stood before General Bendes, who looked surprised as he pointed his gun at the man.

Frank looked at him, then at the inert figure on the floor. They looked exactly alike. C-in-C Bendes appeared to be quite composed.

The man spoke quietly, but clearly.

'We meet again, General. Your plot to take over the USE has failed.'

He smiled. 'I think not,' he pointed at the man and addressed the crowd. 'This is Gunter Von Vernher who has, it seems, escaped from the family mental asylum.' He raised his voice. 'Guards, take him into custody and return him to his cell.'

The guards didn't move.

Now the man smiled. 'You know who I am, General Bendes. I am Count Otto Von Vernher, 'he pointed at the inert body on the floor. 'And that is my brother, Gunter. You had it all worked out: assassinate my brother in full view of hundreds of millions of our people, and then become a military dictator.'

The General raised his voice. 'That is nonsense,' he turned to the troop Commander. 'Arrest this man, he is not Count Otto.'

The Commander didn't move. The regal lady stepped forward.

'This is my husband, Count Otto Von Vernher.'

The Count spoke to the army commander. 'Arrest General Bendes; keep him in solitary confinement while we round up all the other traitors and put them on trial.'

The dumbfounded General was led away. Count Otto stood over his brother shaking his head sadly.

'Commander, take him back to the palace, and sober him up. Treat him gently.'

Ulick was slowly coming around. Frank helped him sit on a chair while the doctor attended to him.

The Count addressed them.

'We have a lot of sorting out to do. The USE is not at war with anyone. The fleet off Aran is now ordered to return to base immediately. All conformity laws are cancelled: what we need is greater originality and local initiative. Where is President Joyc?'

'Here,' Ulick was focusing again.

The Count approached him and shook his hand.

'President Joyc, I've heard a lot about you: I owe you and your friends a great debt of gratitude.'

It was coming to Ulick, slowly, but it was coming.

'Friends? Oh, yes, I have it now.'

'Only for Dan I would still be a prisoner in Mainau castle.'

Dan got up on the counter, lifted Ulick's half full glass and put it on his head. Only Ulick could see him, but millions saw the glass rise by itself empty and return to the counter. Sitting down, Dan burped loudly.

Frank helped Ulick stand up.

'Come on lad, let's go home.'

Prince bounded into the hall, and leapt up on the counter beside Dan.

'Let me introduce you to your new master.' Dan offered.

'No, I'm going to live in the castle with the two ladies and the master.'

'But why?'

'I guess I'm a snob.'

And so it was that peace was restored; the Hibernian delegation returned in triumph to Galway to a real Irish welcome; Ulick resigned as President to spend more time with his beloved Ella; Frank became President and immediately invited Moxy to resume as Taoiseach; the tourists returned to Turla; Meskedra - or whoever he calls himself these days - and Paula lived happily ever after; Prince met a beautiful, full bred bitch and, in due time, found himself surrounded by a family of unruly pups.

THE END

This book has been finished in Madrid
on March, 15th. 2018,

www.ingramcontent.com/pod-product-compliance
Lightning Source LLC
Chambersburg PA
CBHW020344260626
47156CB00004B/1678